GHOSTS OF
CAROLINA COASTS

HAUNTED LIGHTHOUSES, PLANTATIONS, AND OTHER HISTORIC SITES

GHOSTS OF THE

Terrance Zepke

ILLUSTRATED BY JULIE RABUN

PINEAPPLE PRESS, INC.
SARASOTA, FLORIDA

CAROLINA COASTS

*To my brother, who loves ghost stories as much as
I do, and who helped me poke around cemeteries
—even when daylight faded*

Inquiries should be addressed to:
Pineapple Press, Inc.
P.O. Box 3889
Sarasota, Florida 34230
www.pineapplepress.com

Map courtesy of Jim Counts
Photos, unless otherwise indicated, by Terrance Zepke

Library of Congress Cataloging-in-Publication Data

Zepke, Terrance
  Ghosts of the Carolina Coasts: Haunted lighthouses, plantations, and other historic sites / Terrance Zepke ; illustrations by Julie Rabun.– 1st ed.
      p. cm.
  ISBN 1-56164-175-8 (alk. paper)
  1. Ghosts—North Carolina. 2. Ghosts—South Carolina. I. Title.
  BF1472.U6 Z46 1999
  133.1'09759'09146—dc21
                                    98-31815
                                    CIP

ISBN 13: 978-1-56164-175-8 (alk. paper)

First Edition
20 19 18 17 16 15 14 13

Design by Stacey Arnold
Printed in the United States of America

North & South Carolina

CONTENTS

INTRODUCTION

I LOVE THE SOUTH. It's filled with Palmetto trees, wild magnolias, stately old rice plantations, and lots of ghost stories.

I heard my first one at summer camp when I was nine years old. The counselors told us one hair-raising tale after another, trying to scare us silly. Instead, I hung on every word, begging for more. I was hooked.

I've lived in many places, but have spent most of my life in the Carolinas; first in South Carolina and now in Myrtle Beach, South Carolina, and Greensboro, North Carolina. Storytelling is a favorite pastime around here, especially in the Low Country, and I still love to hear a good yarn about things that go bump in the night with no rational explanation. I've spent years listening to and compiling some great tales, and I even learned a few new ones when I was working on *Lighthouses of the Carolinas*, my first book.

Love, greed, murder, and mayhem are the things great stories are made of, and plenty of these elements can be found in the stories collected here. Some of the tales are grounded in library research of old newspaper clippings; the rest are retold as they were recited to me. Some are well known, with many adaptations, and some have seldom, if ever, been heard. I have been told several of these narratives by locals, ranging from young to old, matrons to fishermen. I've included my favorites, and the only change I have made is to adapt some of the language and dialogue to be more contemporary.

As to whether they're true or not is an individual decision. I choose not to explore logical or rational justifications, but to savor

9

the tales as they were meant to be. I hope you will also enjoy them.

And, if at night after you're tucked in bed, reading by the light of your night-table lamp, you hear something in the attic, a not-so-faint creaking or rustling sound, it's probably just the wind sneaking in through a gap around the window, or the effects of an old house settling.

Or is it? Maybe it's the Ghost in the Attic, seeking revenge for his wife's betrayal. Or, maybe it's the spirit of the keeper's wife who was brutally Murdered at Cape Romain by her husband. Maybe she's come looking for him. . . . Or maybe it's a young woman, also known as the Lady in Blue, who is said to appear on particularly dark and stormy nights, warning others to "go back, go back . . ." It could also be the man who was Buried Alive calling to you, trying to get you to open his coffin. . . .

Death gives life its fullest reality.

— Anthony Dalla Villa
April 1987

AT MACO STATION

The single car and train collided with a fatal result. Bits of steel were strewn for up to a mile away. When rescuers dug through the wreckage, they found poor Joe Baldwin's mangled body, but not his head. And, although the search was long and exhaustive, the missing head was never recovered.

It's one of the most intriguing and gruesome stories you'll ever hear. It took place in 1868, at Maco Station (formerly Farmer's Turnout), a stop along the Atlantic Coast Line Railroad (formerly the Wilmington-Manchester-Augusta Railroad). The station was located at Brunswick County's town of Maco, about nineteen miles west of Wilmington, North Carolina. The tiny town's train station was just another stop on the route until one incredible night.

Joe Baldwin was a train conductor on the route that ran back and forth between the coast and nearby inland towns. As his train was pulling into the station that night, Conductor Joe made a devastating realization. The last car had come unhooked and was blocking the tracks where another train was soon due to arrive. In those days, the cars of the wood-burning trains were linked together with couplers and pins. Some of the pins had worked their way loose and fallen off, leaving a solitary car stranded.

Baldwin began to panic, knowing the imminent danger, and he did the only thing he could with such limited time. He seized a lantern and ran to the car platform, where he tried to signal the other train. The brave old conductor heard the engine and knew it was bearing down fast. He leaned over the rail and continued holding the lantern high, moving it up and down and around as much as he dared in a last frenzied effort to warn the conductor.

It is unclear whether the other conductor did not see Joe, or whether he simply did not realize the meaning of the light. Whatever the case, the single car and train collided with a fatal result. Bits of steel were strewn up to a mile away. When rescuers dug through the wreckage, they found poor Joe Baldwin's mangled body, but not his head. And, although the search was long and exhaustive, the missing head was never recovered.

Soon after that tragic night, locals claimed they saw an inexplicable light coming from the swamp around Maco Station. Those who saw it report the white light was about twenty feet above the ground and moved in the same fashion as Joe had frantically swung his signal light. The consensus was the light was Joe Baldwin's spirit, roaming the tracks and swampy area hunting for his head.

The hundreds who have claimed to see the bobbing, eerie light say it is almost impossible to describe. The faint illumination in the distance gets brighter and faster and then zooms by the witnesses and disappears, leaving them wondering what they saw.

Headless Joe Baldwin and the strange illumination became known nationally in 1889 when President Cleveland himself saw the light. The train carrying our nation's leader had to refuel at Maco Station, so the president got off and walked along the tracks. During his walk, he saw two lights and questioned a nearby railroad employee as to why there were two when typically only one signal light is used. The young man answered, "But sir, there is only one light." When President Cleveland persisted he had briefly seen another illumination and pointed in the direction from which it had come, the man slowly nodded knowingly and then told the president the story of one unforgettable night at Maco Station and the resulting mysterious light.

After this, many came to try to explain the vanishing light. They came from across the state and the country, including an investigator from Washington, DC; a Smithsonian Institute research team; a corp of engineers; and even a professor at Duke University. The explanations did not satisfy those who had seen the light. Some of the men said it could be automobile headlight reflections, and the others claimed it was a haze that sometimes forms off of a swamp. Numerous sightings of the light, however, predate the invention of the car! And the ominous glow didn't really resemble swamp haze, or phosphorous gas, as it is scientifically called. Many newspapers and magazines, such as *Life*, were intrigued and pursued the ghostly occurrence, but to no avail.

Drastic measures were finally taken in April of 1964. A German man by the name of Hans Holzer was called. Known as a professional "ghost hunter" and the world's leading authority on ghosts, he was hired to solve the mystery and to bring closure to the Joe Baldwin saga. Author of the book *Ghost Hunter*, Holzer was brought in by the Southeastern North Carolina Beach Association. He was accompanied by his twenty-five-year-old, Austrian-born wife, Catherine Buxhoevden Holzer. Intrigued by the supernatural, she usually traveled with her husband and helped in his research. She certainly attracted further media attention since she was reputedly the great, great, great granddaughter of Catherine the Great and had won an award in New York the previous year for her impressive paintings of ghosts and haunted houses.

They landed at New Hanover County Airport and received a tremendous welcome. The mayor, a band, many citizens of the area, and 1,000 New Hanover High School students carrying lighted lanterns were on hand to hail the arrival of Hans Holzer and his wife. Despite the big production made by the arrival, Hans Holzer

15

came no closer to unraveling the enigma than anyone else did.

A reporter with the *Wilmington Star News*, Charles Joyner, accompanied by a friend and both of their wives, claimed that they all saw the light one night. Mr. Joyner even wrote about it, saying the glow spread about 300 yards and was a few minutes in duration. It reappeared about forty minutes later, again lasting only a few minutes before disappearing for the rest of the night. According to reports gathered by the many witnesses, there didn't appear to be any reason for the light. It was seen at different times of the year, as well as at different times of night. Some soldiers from Ft. Bragg claim they shot bullets at the light, but found no answers.

People continued seeing the strange light, but gave up trying to figure it out. When the station was closed and the tracks were taken up in 1977, the light disappeared. It has never been seen again. Many say it's because Joe Baldwin has finally found his head and can now rest in peace.

Intrigued? For additional information, visit the New Hanover County Public Library in Wilmington.

Devil's Stomping Ground

Less than three hours from the North Carolina coast is Siler City, a wee part of Chatham County. The only noteworthy thing about this small city is the two-hundred-year-old folk story called the "Devil's Stomping Ground."

This area, where many claim the devil comes to play, appears to be a harmless patch of grass, located about one hundred feet off a country road near Siler City's airport. It is a perfect circle, roughly two feet wide and fifteen feet in diameter. The really strange part is what reportedly happens there.

Animals shy away from the area. Women lock their car doors as they drive past. Several people claim to have seen a pair of red, glowing eyes as they passed the road where the circle lies just beyond. It is reported that no one can successfully drive their car over the circle. One man who attempted to disprove this said his car stalled and wouldn't restart. He said the same thing happened when he tried with another car on another night.

Some accounts claim that no one has ever spent the night at the Devil's Stomping Ground. Others say campers have attempted it, but always found themselves well outside of the circle when they awoke. Ethan Feinsilver, a newspaper journalist, decided to see for himself in October 1998. Trying to laugh off the strange accounts as he set up camp with his two big dogs, the reporter admits his imagination was in full gear. However, Feinsilver successfully spent the night inside the circle. The only disturbing thing that occurred during that long evening was the sound of footfalls.

"They weren't loud enough to be someone walking around the tent. They were muffled—sort of ghostly," says Feinsilver. Despite getting a full night's sleep, well, at least a full night's stay, at the Devil's Stomping Ground, the journalist cannot be made to pooh-pooh the existence of something sinister at this site.

BURIED ALIVE

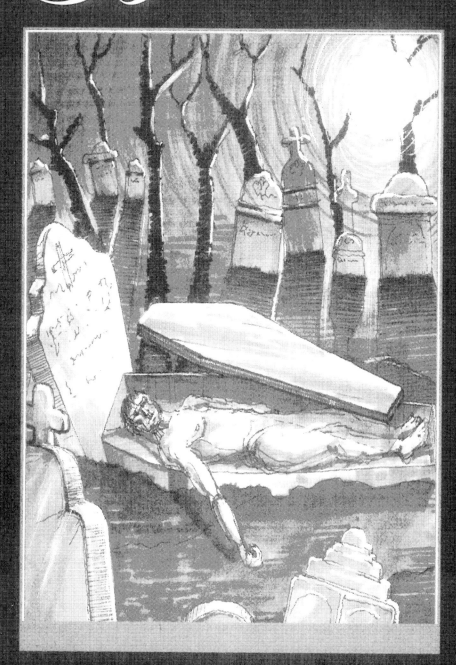

"How could you?" it hissed. "I thought you were my friend. You buried me alive! You buried me alive! Open my coffin and free me."

It was a cruel turn of events. The boy had been out horseback riding, jumping fallen logs and tree branches. What an excellent rider he was! What a wonderful way to pass an afternoon, he thought. Overly cocky, Sam tried to cross a wide hurdle. The horse stumbled and threw him, and he hit his head on a large stone and lost consciousness. When he was found, his parents rushed the young man to the doctor, but it was too late. The physician pronounced him dead.

The young man, barely eighteen years of age when the terrible accident occurred, was buried at Wilmington's St. James Cemetery. His tombstone reads: Samuel R. Jocelyn, 1792-1810.

His best friend since childhood, Alexander Hostler, was overtaken by grief and guilt. If only he had gone riding with him, maybe he could have done something. The death of his friend pulled at his heart and conscience. Alex couldn't sleep for several days after the funeral, as he kept seeing Sam's face every time he closed his eyes. One night, unable to stand it any longer, he decided to visit the grave and say his goodbyes to his longtime friend. He thought maybe that would help him put it behind him and get on with his life. As Alex thought about all the things they would never do together again and how much he missed Sam, a voice interrupted.

"How could you?" it hissed. "I thought you were my friend. You buried me alive! You buried me alive! Open my coffin and free me."

Thinking he had lost his mind, Alex ran out of the cemetery and tried to forget the incident, but Sam's voice plagued the young man day and night. He could get no peace from it. What if they had all made a mistake? Didn't he owe it to his friend to make sure? Knowing no one would believe him, he told only one person, a very close mutual friend, Louis Toomer.

St. James Cemetery, Wilmington, NC

Hysterically, he asked Toomer to go with him to dig up their friend. Although shocked by his friend's plea, he agreed to accompany him since he could see how distraught Alex was. The two waited until well after midnight the following night before going to the gravesite. Upon arrival, Alex fervidly began digging up Sam's plot.

Even though they worked steadily, it took hours to dig up the coffin that had been embedded deep in the earth. When they finally were able to open the coffin, the sight made Louis Toomer cry out in disbelief, while the Alex fell to his knees. Sam's body was face down! When they turned him over, Sam looked much as he had when Alex had last seen him, only his fingernails were different. They were all broken and bloody, obviously from the boy's efforts to open the lid. Scars lined the inside of the coffin around the hinges where Sam had pawed and scraped with all his strength. It must have been a brief struggle, for the boy would surely have quickly suffocated.

The surviving friend was never the same again. He felt he was responsible, although the doctor had said Sam was dead. The senile physician had obviously mistaken unconsciousness for death!

Alexander lost his mental faculties, now diagnosed as a nervous breakdown. From that point on, he spent most of his time at the cemetery pulling up weeds, putting out fresh flowers, and keeping the gravesite in excellent condition.

Many years later, a group of teenagers sneaked into the cemetery. They got more than they bargained for when they stopped at Sam's burial site. Soon after they gathered around the headstone, a muffled voice cried out, "Get off of me! Can't you see I've been buried alive?" Before the frightened and confused kids could figure out what to do, a figure was seen coming towards them. As they scattered among the graves and headed for the gate, they heard the staggering figure exclaim, "I didn't know. I didn't mean to. Please forgive me, Sam, and leave me in peace. . . ."

DEADLY DUEL

"As you are reading this, my time on earth will have expired, for I know I will not survive the duel. You see, I cannot bring myself to aggressively wound or kill my closest friend. I wanted you to know that I loved you. And I do not mind dying if it will show the world this."

*E*lliot was consumed with happiness. His business was doing extremely well, and his sweetheart, Anna, had agreed to be his wife. Thinking his life couldn't get any better, the elated man dashed off a letter to his childhood friend, asking him to be his best man.

Elliot had many friends in Charleston whom he could have asked, but he really wanted Robert to be at his side on his wedding day. If he admitted it to himself, it was partly because he wanted to show off his success. When the boys were growing up, Robert was better at everything. Any sport he undertook he easily mastered. He never seemed to struggle with any subjects in school. On the contrary, he was a scholar, achieving the highest grades in their class. Girls always seemed to bat their eyelashes at him and make up pretenses to flirt with him. But, the amazing part was that Robert seemed ignorant of the endless array of capabilities and charms he possessed.

Elliot's envy didn't prevent him from respecting his boyhood buddy. He was the first to boast about his friend. After all, it took a great deal of guts to strike out on your own the way Robert had, he thought. He had left town to work in a plant up north, and he now owned that plant, as well as two others.

For the first time in his life, Elliot felt on equal footing with Robert. He was now a successful banker and part owner of a textile mill. And, the most beautiful girl in the whole town was going to marry him. Still smiling, Elliot shook himself free of his reflections and finished the letter asking Robert to come meet his fiancée and spend time with them.

Three weeks later, the train delivered Robert to Charleston. The two young men greeted each other enthusiastically.

"It's great to see you Elliot. Congratulations! Now tell me, this must be some girl to want to put up with you for the rest of her life," Robert joked.

"Indeed, she is. I can't wait for you to meet her. As a matter of fact, there is a dance tonight, and you can get to know her then."

That night at the dance, as Elliot scanned the crowd looking for Anna, Robert laid eyes on a beautiful girl wearing an unadorned lilac dress. The simple cut of it showed off her delicate features better than any fancy gown he'd seen a woman wear. As he started to ask his friend for an introduction, Elliot exclaimed, "There she is!" He pushed Robert across the room and as he spun him around to meet Anna, his fiancée, Robert came face to face with the girl in the lilac dress he'd been admiring.

Robert spent the next few days renewing old acquaintances and spending evenings with both his old friend and Anna. Whenever he suggested that just the two school chums do something, Elliot quickly dismissed the idea. The wedding was scheduled to take place the following week, and Robert planned to leave the day after.

He was growing increasingly uncomfortable with the feelings he was having and was anxious for the nuptials and his ensuing departure. That afternoon, Robert received a note from Elliot that would change all of their lives and plans. The note told of the death of Elliot's favorite great uncle and of his need to leave town to attend the funeral. The young man also apologized for having to leave so abruptly and for the unfortunate timing. He promised to be back before the ceremony and requested that Robert tell Anna what had happened.

Robert went to see Anna to share the sad news and to let her know that the groom would be back in time for the wedding to go on as scheduled. The two continued spending time together, as Elliot had also asked. But without Elliot's presence, the pair was unable to deny the strong feelings they'd had since their first meeting. Finally, Robert could stand it no more.

"I think I should leave town. Someone else can serve as Elliot's best man. I don't think I'm suited to the honor, anyway," Robert quietly stated.

"That's probably best," Anna murmured. The two continued staring at each other, consumed with the presence of the other. "But, I don't think I could bear that," she added.

With that simple statement, she had let her feelings be known, and that resulted in a release of emotions Robert could not fight. They talked for hours about what to do. The pair agreed they did not want to hurt Elliot, but they couldn't imagine being apart. Robert felt it was only right he disclose their feelings to his friend. Anna felt it was her duty.

"I do love him. Just not the way I do you," she sadly admitted.

In the end, it was agreed that Robert would deal with Elliot. When Elliot returned to town, Robert told him the wedding was off. He tried to explain how they had fought to deny their feelings, and that no one had wanted, or intended, to hurt him in any way. The words were cold comfort to the man who had been planning to marry in two days' time.

After some time, Elliot spoke. "I believe you when you say you love her. But I too love her, and have loved her long before you knew her. I will not step aside and watch you take the only girl I've ever wanted. But I will be fair, on behalf of the many years we were friends. If you can beat me at a duel, then she is yours. That is the only way."

Robert hesitated before responding. Finally, he spoke, "I don't want to fight you, but I can see you will offer me no alternative. I do want you to know that I wish I had never come back."

"So do I."

With those words, the two parted. The duel was to occur at sunup the next morning. When Anna heard this, she pleaded with both of them not to go through with it, but her words fell on deaf ears. A note was sent to the distraught girl early that morning. It read:

> "My Dearest Anna,
> As you are reading this, my time on earth will have
> expired, for I know I will not survive the duel. You
> see, I cannot bring myself to aggressively wound or
> kill my closest friend. I wanted you to know that
> I loved you. And I do not mind dying if it will
> show the world this."

The note was left unsigned. Who had opted to be the braver man and die rather than kill? Was it Elliot, or her Robert? Out of her mind with fear and guilt, she went looking for the men. She never got the answer to her question, for she could find neither man. The men hadn't called for seconds, so no one had witnessed the duel. The jilted groom-to-be and his former friend were never found.

It is told that on days of wedding ceremonies, when church bells are reverberating throughout Charleston, the spirit of Anna has been seen, perhaps looking for her soulmate.

STAINED GOWN

Looking down, she discovered it came from an arrow firmly embed-
ded in her chest. The girl staggered to the steps, all the while trying to
pull out the arrow. Her mother stood motionless, paralyzed in horror.
Amy made it down a few stairs before she teetered and fell.

Amy was swimming and enjoying the delightful spring afternoon when she heard a splash nearby. The girl saw a young boy about her age swimming just across the shore. She swam over to him and introduced herself.

"I am Concha," he told her.

"Are you an Indian?" she asked. When he nodded, she said, "You don't look like any Indians I have seen. You are lighter skinned, almost white."

"How many of my people do you know?" he joked.

From then on the pair were friends, but they met secretly since her parents would never have allowed her to have any kind of relationship with an Indian.

They spent many days together as they grew up, fishing, swimming, playing, and talking. As the two got older, they fell in love. The forbidden love forced Amy to lead two lives, and she continued the clandestine meetings until the Indian could stand it no more.

"I want to be with you, my love," he proclaimed one day as

they sat under a tree enjoying each other's company.

"You are with me," she answered.

"No, I am not. Not the way I want to be," he quietly replied.

Amy sat up and studied his handsome, tanned face and his intense dark brown eyes, which did not blink as he looked at her. The look he held startled her. The girl jumped up and laughingly challenged Concha to a race. The conversation was forgotten as they chased one another.

Upon arriving home, she found Paul Grimball on her doorstep. He was a nice boy she had danced with many times at parties. He had also walked her home a few times and sometimes came by her house to visit. Amy liked Paul, for he was a good dancer and was always considerate and attentive, but she could hardly believe her ears when Paul told her he had come by to ask her father for her hand in marriage.

"I love you and promise to make a good life for us," he said as he held her hand. Stunned, she silently sat and listened to his words.

When she entered the house, her mother was waiting. "Isn't it wonderful?" she asked her daughter.

"But mama, I am not sure I am ready for such a commitment as marriage."

"It is time to marry and start a family of your own. Paul Grimball is a decent man who comes from a very good family. He will make a fine husband and take care of all your needs."

After this, wedding plans seemed to consume the girl's life. When she was finally able to sneak away to see Concha, Amy found him catching fish.

"Concha, I have something to tell you. I am . . . getting married."

The Indian whirled around in disbelief. "You cannot. We belong together. You do not love him."

"But I can never be with you. We can never have more than this, and that is no life," she sadly replied.

"You do not love him. We belong together. You cannot marry

this man," he repeated softly as he walked away. Amy cried as she watched him disappear from view.

The day of her wedding dawned bright and beautiful. As the unsuspecting girl readied for the ceremony, the Indian sat patiently perched on a tree branch outside her bedroom. He watched as Amy's mother put a strand of pearls around her daughter's neck and then admired the effect. The young woman made a lovely bride in her intricately designed and beaded white gown, which boasted a high collar and fitted waist. Amy's mother kissed her child on the cheek and then picked up the train of the beautiful wedding dress. Amy grabbed her veil and started out of the room. As she walked by the window on her way downstairs, she felt a sharp stab of pain. Looking down, she discovered it came from an arrow firmly embedded in her chest.

The girl staggered to the steps, all the while trying to pull out the arrow. Her mother stood motionless, paralyzed in horror. Amy made it down a few stairs before she teetered and fell. The noise brought her family to the hallway where they rushed to help the young bride, but she was already dead. They didn't know it, but her life had been taken by her one true love.

The Indian was later found on the ground outside the dead girl's bedroom. He had taken his life by flinging himself from the huge tree to the ground far below. Perhaps he thought that the only way they could be together was in death.

The blood-soiled carpet was taken up in the entry, and the blood traces were scrubbed from the steps. The tree was chopped down immediately after the tragedy. In its place, beautiful rhododendron bushes were planted in memory of the child bride. They died within a few months, and nothing has ever lived that was planted where the tree once stood. It seems appropriate that instead of blooming bushes, a large, bare area of dirt will serve to remind us of the Indian and his unconsummated love.

LADY IN BLUE

The storm gave way to a hurricane, and rain pelted against the big glass panes of the watch room and lantern area. Wind accompanied it and circled the tower like an angry force unleashing itself. Thunder and lightning crashed and filled the sky, while waves furiously slapped the shore.

She was a sweet young girl, sixteen years of age. The child's big blue eyes and cherublike face were framed by a mane of golden hair. She lived with her father, her mother having passed away during childbirth. He was the sole keeper of Hilton Head Lighthouse, a rather large responsibility. The man was very conscientious, which was reflected by the many citation medals awarded him by the Light House Board.

The channel and sound surrounding the uninhabited island made it a treacherous route for mariners on their way to other North and South Carolina ports, as well as those crossing by Georgia en route to Florida. To keep the light at optimum operating level, he spent his days making sure the lamp's wicks were cleaned and properly trimmed and the lamp and lantern rooms' windows spotless. Every evening he faithfully hauled buckets of oil from the nearby shed and up the multitude of steps to the lantern room to keep the light burning brilliantly until daybreak.

One night after supper he told his daughter he was going to

check the light, just as he did every night. Within minutes, a storm had arrived at the island. The storm gave way to a hurricane, and rain pelted against the big glass panes of the watch room and lantern area. Wind accompanied it and circled the tower like an angry force unleashing itself. Thunder and lightning crashed and filled the sky while waves furiously slapped the shore. One of the windows shattered from the force of the gale, causing the lamp to flicker. The keeper covered the hole as best he could, and he then spent hours running up and down the stairs to relight the wick or bring more fuel, until he was out of breath and a deep pain filled his chest.

By this time, his daughter had awakened and was frightened by the fierce storm and the absence of her father. She grabbed a dress out of her closet and put on her coat. As quickly as her feet would carry her she crossed the walkway that led from the house to the beacon. There the girl found her father slumped over a step. Despite her crying and begging, he didn't awaken.

The storm had hit the area hard, and it was a couple of days before anyone came out to the island to check on the family. What they found was a tragic sight. Father and daughter were on the tower steps, both dead. She was wearing a pretty blue dress, and he was clutching a lantern and oil bucket. It was later determined the poor man had suffered a heart attack and the girl had died from the shock and trauma.

From that night on, whenever a terrible storm is approaching, a young woman wearing a blue dress has been seen warning others of the impending danger and signaling with her arms and hands to "go back . . . go back. . . ."

One couple even claims to have picked up a young, blond-haired girl wearing a simple blue dress and worn coat soaked from the rain. As the man drove, his wife turned around to talk to the girl, but no one was there! The Lady in Blue had vanished into thin air. The woman was so upset that the man had to pull over to comfort her and look for the missing passenger. He never found the girl who had gotten into their car, but the back seat had to be wiped down from all the water left by the drenched stranger.

Fast Facts about Hilton Head Lighthouse:

• The lighthouse, built in 1880, was constructed of steel, wood, and cast iron.

• The Hilton Head Lighthouse is one of only a handful of skeletal towers still in existence in America.

• The beacon of the lighthouse is now a centerpiece for the Arthur Hills Golf Course at Palmetto Dunes Resort. This course was specifically designed to include the lighthouse.

BLACKBEARD'S

REVENGE

Furious beyond reason, he had the girl brought to his room. As she stood in front of the tall, swarthy pirate, he gave her another chance to change her mind.

*T*here are many myths surrounding Edward Teach, alias Blackbeard the Pirate. They circulate like ceiling fans on a hot, Southern summer day, especially around Ocracoke Island, where the pirate was killed.

Teach was born in a small, British waterfront town. He started out as a privateer, part of a ship's crew commissioned by Her Majesty. (The only difference between a privateer and a pirate was that a privateer attacked and looted ships' cargoes in the name of his country, while pirates did it purely for fun and greed). After Queen Anne's War against Spain ended, Teach changed his name to Blackbeard and became one of a growing number of buccaneers. He soon distinguished himself by earning the reputation as one of the fiercest pirates of all. He was so feared that he was also known as the "Fury from Hell" and the "Black-faced Devil." The young sea robber plundered the profitable West Indies and Caribbean before discovering the bounties of the New World (eastern United States).

He ended up in North Carolina because he needed a pardon for his "Blockade of Charleston," when the pirate held many prominent citizens hostage, captured the city's port, and then looted several ships' cargoes. While it was an incredible, gutsy endeavor on his part, it was also, without doubt, the biggest haul of the pirate's career.

As hoped, the governor of North Carolina didn't seek retaliation for the buccaneer's actions and did indeed grant him a pardon. From that time until his death, the pirate was then able to do as he pleased in North Carolina without consequence, since he shared his booty with the governor. His "reign of terror" in the Carolinas lasted from 1716 to 1718.

Periodically, he came ashore to get provisions or to blow off steam. Once when he was "visiting" Bath he glimpsed a girl whose beauty was so overwhelming he thought the rum he was heavily consuming must have caused hallucinations. The pirate carried on with his merriment and forgot about the girl until he chanced upon her again.

She had long, curly hair that flowed down her back and fell gently across her shoulders. As if the glorious thick curls didn't enhance her enough, she had piercing blue eyes that were so compelling he almost missed her full, lush lips. He figured they were as soft as her young, untanned skin. Although a connoisseur of women (he had been a groom more than a dozen times), not one had ever affected him as this one did. Blackbeard decided right then and there he must have her at any cost.

He sent for her only to be rewarded with a polite rejection: "While I am flattered at your attentions, sir, I am sure I cannot receive them, for I belong to another. I am engaged to be married in a fortnight. Best wishes, Mary."

Furious beyond reason, he had the girl brought to his room. As she stood in front of the tall, swarthy pirate, he gave her another chance to change her mind. She said she loved the man she was engaged to and looked forward to their nuptials. The pirate seemed to take her words well and began issuing orders and making preparations to set sail. Foolishly, the girl thought that was the end of the matter.

Later that day, a spectacular, engraved gold-and-wood box arrived at her home. When she opened it, she found it contained a finger. A note was next to it saying that was all she'd ever see again of her fiancé, signed by the pirate. Blackbeard didn't lie. The young man Mary was to wed was never seen again.

The pirate knew what he was doing. He knew she would suffer more if he let her live and instead killed the man she loved. The beautiful girl went to pieces, unable to get past the guilt she felt for his death. Fishermen and sea captains, once even a boat full of passengers on a dinner cruise, say they have seen a woman fitting Mary's description down by the docks on the anniversary of the day the couple were to be married.

An even more astonishing end to this tale, if it is true, is that the young lady Blackbeard wanted so badly did indeed marry him. He was so taken by her he never forgot her, and he eventually came back for her. This time he swore off piracy, and Mary Ormond finally accepted his proposal.

Unfortunately, the buccaneer wasn't able to keep his word, returning to the sea and his old ways before long. The young bride used to linger at the docks, waiting for Blackbeard to return. This is the girl allegedly seen, many believe.

CURSED CRYPT

Talking softly to her, he carried her to the house and up to their bed-room while her long gown trailed on the floor. A doctor was summoned, who confirmed what the frightened young man already suspected. His lovely bride had contracted the deadly fever, and nothing could be done for her.

An enormous house, complete with a long-railed porch, an oversized wooden front door, and lots of picture windows, used to sit on the highest bluff of Hilton Head Island. As boats neared the island, the house captured the attention of all onlookers because of its distinct location. It had been erected as the perfect home for a young man, William Baynard, and his wife, and the children they would have that would fill it. During long talks, the engaged couple had planned their dream house along with their future.

After an elaborate wedding ceremony, the newlyweds and guests were transported to the island for a grand reception. The wedded pair were taken to their home by means of a magnificent black carriage with an elegant gold-colored interior. The bride beamed with delight when she saw her new home. She kissed her husband and whispered promises of devotion. The rest of the group soon arrived, and the celebration began.

As the couple was dancing, the groom noticed his bride was sweating profusely. Worried about her condition, he led her to a chair. Before they could reach it, she collapsed. Guests hurried to help, but the young man pushed them away and scooped up his trembling wife. Talking softly to her, he carried her into the house and up to their bedroom while her long gown trailed on the floor.

A doctor was summoned, who confirmed what the frightened young man already suspected. His lovely bride had contracted the deadly fever, and nothing could be done for her.

The husband sat by the bed all night, watching his love slowly die. By morning's light she had taken her last breath, but it was another day before he could bring himself to accept this. He marveled that her beauty was still breathtaking as she lay there in eternal slumber. His anguish was beyond anything he had believed he could feel. The most he could do for his betrothed now was to build a spectacular mausoleum, which would symbolize their love and his loss forever more.

It took many men and several days to build the monument, known as Baynard Mausoleum, as the young man had instructed. Finally it was finished, and her body was sealed inside. Every night from then on the man visited the gravesite, sometimes sobbing violently, other times just sitting with his shoulders drooped and his head in his hands. He never got over her death or considered remarrying. He died within a few years, from a broken heart, many said. The enormous crypt was opened just long enough to place his coffin beside his wife's.

After the Civil War, desperate looters dug up many graves searching for heirlooms wealthy women frequently had buried with them. Some tried to break into the mausoleum, but all met with horrible results. One grave robber was crushed by falling tile from the crypt's roof. One man gained entry, but was accidentally locked inside the vault when the heavy door swung shut behind him. His corpse was found by another marauder. It scared him so much when the bony figure fell out on him, the arms swinging around him as if embracing him, that he had a heart attack and never recovered. From then on, no one dared to disturb the crypt.

The story was well known by this time. However, a few youths took a dare to visit the site one night. Upon their arrival, they found a man and woman already there. Oddly, the couple was sitting in front of the mausoleum, arm in arm. But, as the kids approached, the figures mysteriously vanished!

GHOST IN

THE ATTIC

He went to see the woman and ask her about the bizarre story he'd been told. She looked much older than her age. She was approaching death due to illness and was ready to finally tell the truth.

T hud, thump.

Thud, thump.

Thud, thump.

"It sounds like something being dragged across the floor, doesn't it?" the youngest child asked.

"Don't be silly, honey. It's just something shifting in the attic," the father reasoned as he and his wife exchanged looks.

By week's end, the family had unpacked and settled in, comfortable in their new dwelling. The family, who had moved so the father could take a better job, felt very fortunate to have gotten the nice, big house at such a good price.

Their happiness was dampened by the continuous sounds in the attic. Even the father became nervous as they persisted nightly. But, whenever he entered the attic to explore the source of the peculiar noise, nothing suspicious was ever found.

A few months later, the oldest boy came home with a story

he'd heard at school about the former occupants of their house. "The previous owner was a man who stole some valuables from his employer and then abandoned his family. That's our ghost!" he exclaimed. "Don't you see? He can't rest in peace because of his guilty conscience, so his spirit rattles and thumps around in our attic."

The excited boy took a deep breath and continued, "After he ran off, the woman wanted to get out of town and out of the house in a hurry, so she sold it for less than it was worth. She lives in a neighboring town with her two kids."

The father felt he had no choice but to go see the woman and ask her about the bizarre story he'd been told. She looked much older than her age. She revealed she was approaching death due to illness and was finally ready to tell the truth.

"I was anxious to sell the house and leave town, but not because of the gossip—because of the ghost! The ghost of my dead husband inhabits that house. He didn't run off. I killed him. I realize my confession shocks you, but you have to understand the circumstances. You see, when we married twelve years ago, my husband promised me a wonderful life. A life full of comfort and security. He told me I would be a woman of means, if I just stuck by him. Well, I did, for what it was worth. We both had been working for a rich family since three days after we married. Twelve years of cleaning their big, fancy house and seeing to all their needs. Twelve years, and my sorry husband had accomplished nothing! Worse still, he didn't even seem interested in trying anymore. I was tired of it.

"I talked him into helping me steal some valuables from our employers. I knew they would miss them and who they'd accuse. I told my husband to hide them in our attic and he did. Only, while he was doing that, I hit him on the head with a cooking pot, bolted the door, and left him up there. I had sent my children to a relative's for a visit.

"When I was certain he must be dead, I went up into the attic.

I found his corpse next to the heavy old steamer trunk full of stolen items. It was something seeing him sprawled out, like he was taking a long nap or something.

"I carefully tore out an attic wall and sealed my husband in it. Then I told everyone that he had run off. So, when the valuables were reported missing, it looked like my husband had taken them and abandoned his family. Everyone in town felt so sorry for me since I had been deserted by my husband, with two children and forced to sell my house at any cost.

"Until the house sold, I continued living in it, packing everything up and making arrangements to move. During that time I began hearing noises coming from the attic. I only heard them when I went to bed at night, but they kept me awake all night long. I heard the thumping and pounding every night until I left the house.

"I made myself go up there and remove the jewels and heirlooms from that trunk. Slowly and carefully, I've sold them and used the money to live on. You know at first, I never gave a thought to what I'd done. Twelve years of anger and bitterness eating away at a person can drive them to crazy, foolish acts. But, it finally dawned on me that I had killed my husband.

"I haven't known peace since then. I've tried everything. I left that house. I left that town. I even tried to talk to his spirit to say how sorry I was, but he pervaded my life. You may not believe this, but I have regretted what I did. But, regrets don't make things different. I have never been able to enjoy the money, or my life, since my husband's death. I think his spirit still roams that attic, unable to be a part of this world anymore, but unwilling to fully accept death."

The house was later destroyed by an accidental fire. No one knows if the dead man's body was excavated prior to this.

MAN IN THE

GRAY SUIT

Suddenly, the carriage slid toward the edge of the road, due to the impact of the wind mixed with increasingly heavy mud. As the driver tried to rein in the horses, they careened again. This time the wind and mud were enough to take them off the road. The carriage turned over a few times as it plummeted down the big embankment.

The carriage was on its way from Pawleys Island to Murrells Inlet. As the young man bounced along inside the buggy, he pondered all the events that had led to this day.

He had met the girl more than a year and a half ago and had fallen in love with her instantly. Not more than two months after that his mother had taken ill. Eventually, it was decided all that could be done for her had been attempted. The doctor suggested taking her to Europe, where more sophisticated treatments were available.

The wealthy plantation owner asked his only son to escort his mother on the journey, as it was nearly harvest time and he could not get away. The young man asked his love to wait for him:

"I will be back as soon as possible, and then I want us to become man and wife."

His mother slowly improved and was finally able to travel and return home. During the boat ride home, they excitedly made plans for his future.

The girl had waited for him and quickly said yes to his proposal. Unfortunately, on the day they were to marry, a terrible storm occurred. For the last five days the weather had been the same. The skies remained dark, the ground stayed wet, and the roads were thick with mud from the downpour. The groom had considered postponing the ceremony until the foul weather cleared, but he just couldn't bear the thought of another long night without his true love beside him. He and his bride-to-be had decided to go ahead with the wedding ceremony in spite of the weather.

His thoughts turned to her during the tedious, rough ride. He knew she would be a stunning bride, and he hoped she would be equally pleased at his appearance. He had carefully selected a fashionable gray suit, tailored especially for him.

As the carriage slowly progressed towards the church, the atmospheric conditions worsened. As he looked out the window, the young man hoped his family would be able to make it. They were coming later in the day, with hopes that the heavy rain would slacken by then. The father had tried to get his son to go with them, but the groom was too anxious to sit around and wait and had gone ahead in his own carriage.

Suddenly, the carriage slid towards the edge of the road due to the impact of the wind mixed with increasingly heavy mud. As the driver tried to rein in the horses, they careened again. This time the wind and mud were enough to take them off the road. The carriage turned over a few times as it plummeted down the big embankment. The impact of the fall killed both the driver and the groom-to-be.

Today, along the roads around Pawleys Island and Murrels Inlet many locals claim to have seen a young man wearing a gray suit. He appears just before a fierce storm or hurricane hits the area to warn people of the approaching danger. It is also said that anyone who sees the man in the gray suit will come to no harm.

$\mathcal{B}$ODY IN

A BARREL

To his great distress, they were nowhere near land. By his calculations, it would be another three weeks before they reached any civilization.

Captain Silas Martin had two great loves—the sea and his family. Unfortunately, his love of the sea and the livelihood he earned from it often required him to leave his wife and daughter. The mariner, however, came home whenever possible and stayed as long as he could. He always brought his child something he had picked up during the voyage, such as a model ship or a wood carving.

The little girl worshipped her father. Whenever he was due home, she would wait for hours at the living room window, watching for him to come up the path to the front door. As soon as she saw him, the child always ran as fast as she could outside to hug and greet her father. When it was time for the man to leave again, his daughter always begged to go, and the mariner always promised to take her along when she was old enough.

Finally, on her thirteenth birthday, Captain Martin consented to let the youth accompany him on a trip to the West Indies. His wife was understandably concerned that her daughter's first trip was such a big journey, but repeated assurances by her husband, combined with her child's nonstop pleading, made the mother relent.

Once on the boat, the girl stood on the deck watching the shoreline become more and more faint until it disappeared from view. She was so jubilant about the sea voyage that her heart pounded furiously most of the day. The first part of the trip was extremely pleasant, and she was having the best time. Her father even let her take the wheel and guide the vessel as he looked on. As they passed Florida and continued towards the Caribbean, however, the seas became much rougher. The boat tossed terribly because of the high waves breaking over its sides. It was all the crew could do to keep the ship afloat and on course. It was one of the worst voyages Captain Martin had ever made.

The child got ill from the constant rocking of the vessel. She was unable to eat. She could keep nothing down, not even broth. Finally, the storms passed. Unfortunately, they discovered that either all of the drinking water had become contaminated during the storms, or the water bottles had broken during the incessant tossing and pitching of the vessel. There were no liquids aboard, save some jugs of wine and barrels of rum, neither of which were suitable to give to the dehydrated girl for fear of dehydrating her more. She began to sweat and run a temperature, a small one at first that gave way to a raging fever.

The sea captain could do nothing for his only child. He felt helpless as he held his daughter's hand, lay rags of sea water on her head, and carried her up to the deck. He hoped fresh air might help, but the girl just convulsed in his arms. Out of desperation, the father tried many things, but nothing seemed to help.

They were nowhere near land. Battling the storms had cost them a great deal of time. By his calculations, it would be another three weeks before they reached any civilization. The youth simply was not strong enough to hold on until then.

Knowing his wife would never forgive him if he didn't bring the child home for a proper funeral, the man put the dead girl in a rum barrel, "pickling" her until he could get back from the West Indies.

Once home, her small frame was removed from the barrel and placed in Wilmington's Oakdale Cemetery during a small funeral service.

A spirit now fills the former residence of Captain Silas Martin, 321 South Fourth Street. A muffled voice is sometimes heard coming from the old bedroom of the deceased girl, but no one has ever been able to find the source of the voice, or to figure out what is being said.

Most people think it's the soul of the father, cursing himself for the death of his only child. It's believed he frequents the old bedroom of the child, when he isn't at the cemetery visiting the grave.

Note: The child's cause of death varies, according to the storyteller. This version is more common, but some cite yellow fever as the cause of death, while some simply state that it is unexplained.

MURDER AT

CAPE ROMAIN

Almost insane with despair and fear, the woman grabbed up the box holding her gold and jewels from the mantle behind her. She flung open the door and bolted out of the house into the storm.

*I*t was no secret the strapping Norwegian had a temper, but no one suspected just how violent it was. Perhaps that's because as a lighthouse keeper, Fischer led a solitary existence. Just he and his wife were stationed at one of South Carolina's most remote locations, Cape Romain.

Discovered by Spanish explorers in the sixteenth century, it is as dangerous and remote today as it was then because of the nine miles of ever-shifting sandbars that surround the isle. No one ever visited Cape Romain due to its inaccessibility. Until recently, the island wasn't near any civilization. Supplies were obtained only a few times a year when a ship, on its way to Charleston or Georgetown, would anchor as far inland as possible, and then the keeper would row out to pick up the provisions.

Fischer stayed busy fishing, hunting, taking care of the house, and readying the light for each night's vigil. It was a tough, but peaceful and good life, he thought. His wife cooked and cleaned and tended the garden. It was a lonely, tedious, and not-so-good life, in her opinion.

One night, while they were eating dinner, she broached the subject of going home to Norway to visit her family.

"This is our home now!" he growled.

Frightened by his tone, she let the matter drop. But as summer turned to fall, and then to winter, she could take it no more. When her husband came in for his evening meal, she told him she wanted to go home and see her family.

The old and new Cape Romain light towers as they appear today
—surrounded by an overgrown refuge and as desolate as ever.

Again he bellowed, "This is your home now."

But this time she didn't back down. "This God-forsaken place may be your home, but it's not mine. I miss my family and my homeland and I intend to go."

With that the keeper's eyes squinted at her until they were almost closed. "I am your husband and you will honor my wishes. We will talk of this no more."

As a storm was brewing in the small four-room house, it was

also taking place outside. Tree limbs shook terribly from the whipping winds, while the tides got higher and higher. The horizon was a blanket of darkness, except for periodic streaks of lightning.

The woman softened her voice, but continued speaking. "It is my money, left to me by my first husband upon his death. This trip is very important to me. And I want to leave at week's end," she timidly squeaked out as she stared back at the big, angry man who little resembled the person she thought she'd married.

He stood up abruptly, accidentally knocking over the chair he had been sitting in.

Almost insane with despair and fear, the woman grabbed the box holding her gold and jewels from the mantle behind her. She flung open the door and bolted out of the house into the storm. She ran for a long time before dropping to the ground. Once on her knees, she hysterically began digging up the earth with her bare hands. Despite the pelting rain, the woman continued until she felt she had dug far enough. Finally, she threw the box into the hole, buried it, and then reluctantly headed back to the house.

When she neared the dwelling, she could see a figure looming against the doorway, obviously waiting for her. By this time, his anger had mounted to a point where he couldn't think, and the sight of his disobedient wife furthered his fury. The keeper moved out of the way and allowed her to enter. What he did after that is unthinkable.

He opened a kitchen drawer and pulled out the biggest knife it contained. Next, he crossed the room in almost a single stride and quickly stuck it in the woman's chest. The keeper swung the blade several times until he realized what he was doing and then dropped the knife. But by this time, he had already killed her. When the storm subsided, he dug a hole big enough for the corpse. Fischer put the body in it, shoveled the loose dirt on top of his dead wife, and marked the grave.

He told everyone it was suicide. The Norwegian said his wife had been despondent for some time, but that he thought she would get over it. A true story, except for the ending. No one ever questioned it or found out the truth until Fischer confessed on his deathbed.

Keepers stationed at Cape Romain from then on tended the poor woman's grave. One such keeper was Fredrich Wichmann (who served as keeper at the Cape Romain Lighthouse for twenty-one years), whose son tells of many nights when they heard footsteps on the stairs to the half story above. Neither the father nor his son ever found anyone when they investigated the sounds. And, although the floorboards had been repeatedly scrubbed until clean of her blood, drops of blood always reappeared. They could be seen until the lighthouse was decommissioned and the cottage was destroyed.

No one knows what happened to the buried gold and jewels.

Fast Facts about the Cape Romain Lighthouses:

• The two towers are a rare exception to the twin-tower rule, which specified that the original tower was to be destroyed when a second tower was built.

• The lighthouses are part of the 65,000-acre Cape Romain National Wildlife Refuge, established in 1932.

• The Cape Romain lighthouses are located on Lighthouse Island, approximately forty minutes by boat from the nearest town, McClellanville. McClellanville is approximately thirty-five miles north of Charleston (US 17) and thirty-three miles south of Georgetown (US 17). There is a boat launch for private boats located at the town hall. However, the towers are closed to the public and cannot be reached except by wading through water and heavy mud.

Voodoo Woman

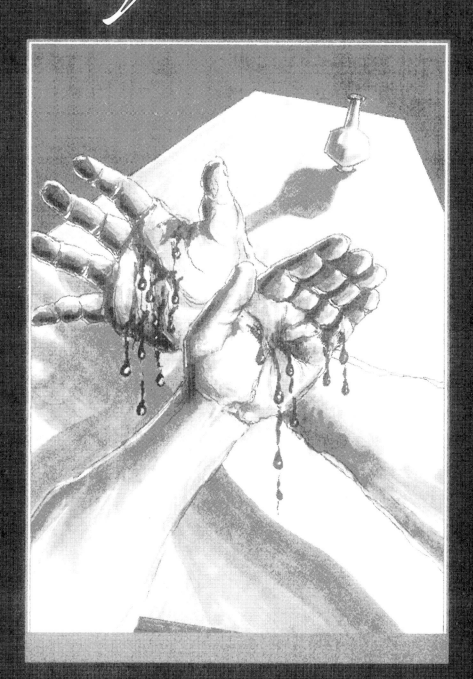

Her black ensemble was filthy and worn. Her unkempt hair was also black, but streaked with gray. The worst thing about her, though, was her smell. An odor of liquor mixed with uncleanliness hung over the voodoo woman.

T his is a disturbing tale about a man who fell in love with a young lady who did not return his interest. He did not possess much money or brains and was not even close to handsome, but he very much wanted this girl.

She worked in a dress shop just across the street from his employment. Every day he tortured himself by watching her through the store's big front window. The weight in his heart got heavier each day, until he came up with a reckless plan, born of his desperation.

He had heard of a woman, said to be half crazy, capable of casting spells and making potions. The gentleman set out before daybreak to find the woman, and by midday had reached Buxton, where she lived. With all his courage, he knocked on the door of the run-down shack. After pounding on the decrepit wood with his fist, it was yanked open by a ghastly-looking old woman.

Her black ensemble was filthy and worn. Her unkempt hair

was also black, but streaked with gray. The worst thing about her, though, was her smell. An odor of liquor mixed with uncleanliness hung over the voodoo woman.

"What do you want?" she croaked as she put her face up to his. He wanted to hop on his horse and get out of there as quickly as possible, but his legs wouldn't move.

"I've come to . . . to buy a love potion," he stammered.

"Bring two bottles of whiskey and come back in three days," she told him. And with that, she slammed the door.

In three days, unsure of what to expect, he again banged on her door. The old witch signaled him inside to what looked like a parlor of black magic. There were a multitude of jars filled with insects and spices, and the young man wasn't sure what else. Strewn about were beads and candles of various sizes and shapes. But his attention became fixed on the item the hag was holding. It was a small vial of yellowish liquid—the love potion!

After they exchanged booze and elixir, the hideous woman gave the lovesick man specific instructions on how to dispense the formula. But when the time came, he was so nervous and excited he couldn't remember what the hag had told him. The fellow swigged down some of the liquid, and then slipped the rest into a cup of tea that he offered the girl. She didn't like him, but she took the tea in hopes that he would soon go and leave her alone.

Whatever was in the potion evidently worked. The girl accepted his dinner invitation and returned his attentions from then on. He was so happy for a while he couldn't believe his good fortune, but then she began to get on his nerves. She wanted to be with him all the time, and when they were together, she either continuously gushed about how much she loved him or questioned what he had been doing since they were last together.

He went back to see the voodoo woman, begging her to reverse the spell. She brushed off his pleas, telling him, "I warned you to be careful. It cannot be undone."

He went home determined to try to make the relationship work, but the young man knew it was doomed because he couldn't even stand the sight of her anymore. Finally, he broke it off.

Unable to accept his rejection, she took her own life in front of him.

"I am already dead inside," she said as she looked him in the eye. Before he could stop her, she pulled out a blade several inches in length and plunged it into herself.

The girl was buried two days later. Mysterious beads of blood kept appearing on the young man's hands. He kept washing them, but the spots came back. As a result, the young man was ostracized by everyone in the town. He even lost his job. His last hope was the witch. Dejectedly, he rode to her shack. When he got there, the hovel stood bare of furniture and vacant of occupants. The only evidence the hag had ever been there was her lingering odor and some empty bottles found out back.

Having no one and nowhere else to turn, he stayed and lived the rest of his days in the dilapidated structure, hidden away from everyone.

5

14 MARKET

The photographer ran into the hall and started snapping pictures. In disbelief, the reporter and photographer raced back to the paper, afraid to share what they had seen with anyone until they looked through the photos.

T he house at 514 Market Street, in historic Wilmington, North Carolina, is haunted. "George," as the resident ghost has been named, is said to be much like Casper the Friendly Ghost—mischievous, but harmless.

The Italian-style house was built in the mid-1800s for Lieutenant Colonel William Jones Price and his family. A couple of nights after they moved in, the family was gathered in the parlor after supper, playing games, talking, and enjoying each other's company. Their activities halted upon hearing thumps and footsteps overhead, but a search of the upstairs revealed nothing suspicious. These unexplainable occurrences happened frequently, at first scaring the family. After a while, though, when no harm came to anyone, they began to listen for and joke about "their ghost."

The antics increased from mysterious noises to objects being moved from their normal positions, almost as if someone were redecorating. Sometimes, the kitchen was messed up in the morning, as if someone or something had been in it deliberately leaving evidence, saying, "Yes, I live here, too!" The children were asked if they had anything to do with it, but they vehemently denied it. The mother and father believed them because the mess did not resemble a childish prank, nor could the children have reached some of the items that had been taken out of the pantry.

Tapping sounds were also heard, as if someone was in the walls, trying to get out. It was these noises that most disturbed the family. They couldn't find a suitable explanation for them. The kids talked it over with their friends, while their parents did the same with shopkeepers and neighbors. The family lived there many years, but they never discovered the cause of the activities. Eventually they moved, and other families lived at the residence on Market Street. The story of the ghost grew until it got the attention of the local newspaper.

A reporter and photographer were dispatched and spent some time in the home with the current occupants' permission. The two sneaked around and peeked into empty rooms, waiting to get a glimpse of the source of all the strange things that had been disclosed. After spending two days there, they were about to give up when they heard someone running in the upstairs hall. They looked at each other and hurried to the stairway. When they got upstairs, the men found a bedroom rocking chair moving back and forth as if someone had just gotten out of it. No one was home except the mother, who was in the kitchen, and there was no draft or breeze that would have propelled the chair.

As the newsmen pondered the incident, a swishing sound caught their attention. The photographer ran into the hall and started snapping pictures. In disbelief, the reporter and photographer raced back to the paper afraid to share what they had seen with anyone until they looked through the photos. After the film was developed, they each held their breath as they studied the images. The first couple revealed nothing extraordinary, but the third and final photograph showed a ghostly presence or apparition, as the image did not have the figure or body of a human being.

For many years, the dwelling housed the Chamber of Commerce, making the old Price-Gause House a perfect setting to introduce visitors to the charms and lore of this major port city. Today, the Chamber of Commerce staff has moved to a bigger facility, but longtime employees of the chamber recall unexplained pranks and office incidents. These include faucets, typewriters, and lights mysteriously being turned on. "George" apparently loves a good pipe, as the pungent aroma that accompanies one was often prevalent, as well as the smell of sweet potatoes baking.

And according to an old newspaper article, a former director of the Chamber of Commerce, Joe Augustine, claims "George" has been investigated by a spiritual analyst and was found to be ". . . a man depicted without a brain, without vision in his eyes—a moon-mad man . . . with a triple personality."

Before that, members of the Gause family lived with the ghost. They said "George" was active mainly at night: making himself heard in the attic, thumping or tapping on the walls, rocking in a rocker, messing up beds by unmaking them, and leaving dirty silverware and napkins in the kitchen—maybe after a late-night snack of sweet potatoes.

The three-story structure is now owned by a local architectural firm, which has restored the historic structure to use as office space. Apparently, neither the renovations nor the new occupants disturbed "George." BMS Architects' employees claim the front door opens when no one is there. His footsteps are heard so often on the steps that no one even looks up anymore. The strong smell of a pipe being smoked permeates the office, as well as the aroma of sweet potatoes browning in the oven. But, even more eerie than all of these unexplained noises and odors is the overpowering feeling of an unseen presence.

Intrigued? You can read more about this in the Star News *(Wilmington, NC), Section D of the October 29, 1967, edition (New Hanover County Public Library, Wilmington, NC).*

JEALOUSY

DOESN'T BECOME HER

Not long after the marriage, Sheila took ill. Her young husband brought her home to her family. Her sister spent many hours reading, visiting, and caring for Sheila. The big, bright wedding band often caught the light and seemed to dance in front of the older girl's eyes. She became obsessed with it.

*T*his is the tale of two sisters from Avon, North Carolina. We'll call them Sheila and Martha, although their real names are unknown. They got along well as children, sharing toys and dolls and fantasizing about the men they would one day marry. As they grew up, it was apparent that Sheila was the best looking in the family, with a perfect complexion and captivatingly large brown eyes. Martha was a mannerly woman, but short on looks and personality. The charming and easygoing younger sibling had many offers of marriage, but couldn't commit to anyone until her older sister was betrothed, as was the custom in those days.

The girls' father arranged for the son of the town's new banker to come to dinner. He had hopes this boy would be interested in settling down with his eldest child, as the young man was quiet and also rather plain in appearance. His hopes seemed answered when the boy called several times after that night. To the father's chagrin, he soon discovered it wasn't his older daughter the boy was interested in, but his youngest, Sheila.

The boy professed his love for Sheila to her father. He told him that he would do anything to make her happy. He begged for her hand in marriage, and the sympathetic father acquiesced. He was afraid his older, introverted daughter might never marry, and he didn't want both his children to be spinsters.

Sheila accepted his proposal, for she had fallen for the gentle, soft-spoken young man. They wed only six months from that day. At the ceremony, the groom put a gorgeous gold-and-emerald wedding band on his betrothed's finger.

The couple seemed truly happy together until Sheila became ill with malaria. The distraught young man brought her home to her family, where care and attention could be given around the clock. Martha spent many hours reading, visiting, and caring for her sick sister. The big, bright ring that encompassed Sheila's finger often caught the light and seemed to sparkle and dance teasingly in front of the older girl's eyes. She became obsessed with it.

When her sister passed on, she started to summon her parents, but then hesitated. Instead, she tried to yank the wedding ring off of her dead sister's finger and to place it on her own. At first the gold ring didn't come off, as it was a little small for Sheila's finger. It had needed to be resized, but once Sheila had put it on, she wouldn't allow it to be taken off. Tugging so hard to get the ring off, one of Martha's fingernails pricked Sheila's skin and drew blood. Martha quickly stopped the bleeding and rubbed all traces of blood away. She then cut herself in her hurried attempt to slip the jeweled band on her finger before she was caught. Martha had been more jealous of her sister than she had realized. She justified her behavior with the thought that the wedding ring should have been hers all along as the first born.

Her parents sent for the husband. While they were waiting for him, Martha realized she wanted more than the ring. She wanted to marry the widowed man. In his depressed and vulnerable state, she would make him realize he needed her to take care of him. It took so long to locate and summon the young man, Martha was able to work out all the details of her scheme to accomplish this. Before he could arrive and she could set her plan in motion, the girl took terribly ill and died.

Her jealousy cost the girl her life. Getting the ring off her dead sister's finger had brought about her death, because in her haste to get it off she had mixed the woman's poisoned blood with her own.

A ghost continues to be seen around the Cape Hatteras area. It is popularly believed to be the younger sister looking for her missing wedding ring.

KEEPER'S

DAUGHTER

Suddenly, the clouds broke and the rain came. At first it was only sprinkling, but the rain grew harder and faster, pushing the waves over the small boat's sides.

North Island lies where Winyah Bay meets the Atlantic Ocean. A seventy-two foot beacon was erected on the island to aid navigation for ships en route to South Carolina's third biggest port, Georgetown. Unlike North Island, Georgetown was a booming and bustling place, filled with antebellum-style plantations. At one time the town served as the world's leading exporter of rice and indigo. Today, many of these impressive estates can still be seen by those boating the Intracoastal Waterway.

For many years, a keeper and his daughter were the only occupants of North Island, so they had to row over to Georgetown for supplies, or just to see other human faces. The keeper always took his daughter, as she liked to see the pretty things in the shop windows and talk to some of the interesting people that resided in the town. The woman who owned the confectionery shop always gave her a sweet when she stopped in, and an old sea captain told her stories of faraway places and people while holding her in his lap and patting her on the head.

The keeper had to time his trips into town carefully to miss low tide, but still get back before it was time to light the tower's lamp. Today he was a little concerned about the dark clouds and sky overhead, but figured they could make it home if they hurried. He loaded his little girl and provisions into the dingy and started out. The keeper rowed as fast as he could as he noticed the skies becoming more menacing-looking.

Suddenly, the clouds broke and the rain came. At first it was only sprinkling, but the rain grew harder and faster, pushing the waves over the small boat's sides. The little girl tried to bail out the water while her father rowed on. Suddenly, a big wave hit the boat and knocked it on its side. The child catapulted out of the craft. The terrified father jumped in after her, calling her name and searching for her until he was exhausted. Just as he could endure no more, he found her, barely breathing, but alive.

Some fishermen, also caught in the storm, saw them and picked them up.

"Thank you! Thank you for saving me and my daughter," the father cried as he gave into his fatigue and fell fast asleep. The men looked at each other but said nothing.

When the keeper awoke, he was in an unfamiliar bed. As soon as he gained his strength, he got up and wandered out the door. One of the fishermen who had rescued the keeper and his daughter arose from a chair and asked him how he felt.

"Still a little dazed, but all right. I'd like to check on my daughter now, if you don't mind," he added.

The fisherman explained how they had found him and pulled him into their boat, but that the keeper was alone when they helped him.

"You mentioned a daughter before you passed out, but we thought you were delirious from the trauma as there was no sign of anyone else around your dingy."

"My daughter was with me—we were heading back to the lighthouse after spending the day in town. Oh God!" The father sank into a chair as he realized what had happened. "I must have imagined that we were both rescued, not wanting to believe the truth. I must not have saved her! I let my only child drown!"

The keeper was inconsolable. He never got over the loss of his daughter, and he never left North Island again. Local fishermen brought him supplies and checked on him. After his death, boaters began seeing a man and little girl rowing around the island. Whenever their boat got close, the dingy and its occupants disappeared. People who knew the story of the keeper's daughter headed to shore as soon as they saw the boat containing the man and little girl, for they knew the apparition meant that a severe storm was coming.

Fast Facts about the Georgetown Lighthouse:

The Georgetown Lighthouse (also known as the North Island Lighthouse) was orginally built in 1801. It was rebuilt in 1812 and again in 1867 after it suffered damage due to the Civil War. The unmanned beacon runs day and night since it lacks a timing mechanism. North Island, the site of the tower, is a deserted, fifteen-mile-long wildlife refuge. Land has been cleared around the lighthouse, but the rest of the refuge remains untouched.

SPIRIT OF

THEODOSIA

Early one morning, her husband kissed her good-bye and watched the boat take her away. She was never seen again, and no one knew what had happened until many years later.

Aaron Burr accomplished what most men only dream about. He became one of the top leaders of this country when he was elected the third vice president of the United States. Yet, few would want to have lived his life.

Burr started out as part of General George Washington's staff. Later he was elected to state assembly, then appointed attorney general. Next he won a seat in the United States Senate. To win the election, he had used unscrupulous political tactics to defeat opponent General Philip Schuyler, who was Alexander Hamilton's father-in-law. This made Burr a permanent and bitter rival of Alexander Hamilton.

In 1800, both Aaron Burr and Thomas Jefferson ran for president on the Republican ballot. There was a tie, and in the competition that followed, Alexander Hamilton used every political favor he was owed to see to it that Jefferson, and not Burr, became President of the United States.

Blaming Hamilton for ruining his chance at the presidency,

Vice President Burr challenged him to a duel. On July 11, 1804, at Weehawken, New Jersey, Aaron Burr killed Alexander Hamilton during this well-known duel. With warrants issued for his immediate arrest, Burr contacted an old army buddy and was quickly smuggled out of the country.

His only daughter, Theodosia, was forced to say goodbye to her father, whom she was very close to, when she was barely a grown woman. She wed South Carolina governor Joseph Alston, and they made a life together. But as the years advanced, she continued to miss her father terribly. Willing to do anything for his wife, Governor Alston arranged for Theodosia to visit her exiled father. The rendezvous was carefully, secretly arranged. A boat was chartered to take her to New York where she would meet her father, and then the two would take a cruise vessel the rest of the way to his home in France.

Early one morning, her husband kissed her goodbye and watched the boat take her away. She was never seen again, and despite a massive investigation, no one found out what had happened until many years later.

As the boat passed North Carolina's Bald Head Island, it was attacked by pirates. During the skirmish the crew was killed, and the boat was sunk. Only Theodosia was left alive. When the group's leader discovered the young woman, he began to taunt her.

"I am not afraid of you, or your savage crew!" she shouted at him. "If I am to die by your hand, it will be without so much as a single tear shed."

The pirate almost smiled at those words. Maybe he would enjoy her company for a short while before he disposed of her, he mused.

The pirate left her at Bald Head Island while he went to hide his loot. The buccaneer, promising to be back by nightfall, left a trusted member of his crew to keep an eye on the enchanting woman. Theodosia watched as the grubby-looking man easily consumed a bottle of whiskey. Within a couple of hours, he was asleep.

She knew this was her only chance to escape, but what to do? She could hide, but for how long? She had no food or survival skills. Besides, it would only delay the inevitable, and then what? She would surely be tortured and killed, or forced to please a tribe of despicable pirates.

I cannot endure that, she thought. The chances of a boat landing on the deserted island in time to rescue her were almost none. Night was approaching, and the rest of the pirates would be returning at any time. Theodosia took a deep breath and walked bravely into the surf.

When the guard awoke, he found himself alone. He lit a lantern, and while he was frantically searching the area, the rest of the pirates returned and learned what had happened. The crew searched the entire island but were unable to find the girl. The only trace of her was a hair ribbon found near the water and footprints leading into the surf. Realizing she must have drowned herself, the captain tortured his first mate and then forced him to meet his death the same way she had.

Years later, some of that crew was heard telling the story of Theodosia Burr Alston's capture, and of that night on Bald Head Island. The story may explain the apparition seen sometimes at the water's edge when the moon is full. The figure may be Theodosia on her way to her death, or the pirate guard who followed her.

CRY OF THE

WOUNDED SOLDIER

The next owners were the Altaffers, who were not told about the ghost prior to moving into the house. Their "introduction" to Keefer was through their little boy, Lawrence. The child told his parents he had seen and talked to a man in a blue uniform.

Now Bern was occupied during most of the Civil War, making it a place of great historical significance. Over 145 historic structures are still in existence in New Bern. Not only do they still stand, the buildings and homes have all been restored and are immaculately maintained as businesses or residences.

These historic dwellings were taken over during the War Between the States and used as hideouts, headquarters, or hospitals. As a result, each building has an interesting story or two to go along with it.

This tale centers around the Jerkins-Richardson house, built circa 1848–1849, which was seized and used as a hospital for Union soldiers. During this time, many soldiers came and went, as their wounds healed or they died. One brave soldier named Keefer, who was seriously injured, spent an extended amount of time at the house before he died from his wounds.

Since that time, the house, particularly the second-floor rear bedroom on the northeast corner, has been haunted by his spirit. His method of haunting varies according to the families who have resided in the Jerkins-Richardson House.

The Evans are one of the families who have encountered the Union soldier while living in the house. All the members of the Evans family, with the exception of Dr. Evans, claim to have seen the Union soldier. Dr. Evans' daughter often found items from her dresser neatly arranged on the floor. Later, both she and her husband say they saw the ghost standing at the foot of the bed one night.

The next owners were the Altaffers, who were not told about the ghost prior to moving into the house. Their "introduction" to Keefer was through their little boy, Lawrence. The child told his parents he had seen and talked to a man in a blue uniform. During the Altaffers' time in residence at the Jenkins-Richardson House, Lawrence was the only family member to see the spirit.

Next, the DeCamps moved in. Mrs. DeCamp swore that every time she closed the rear bedroom door she would return to find it open. Mrs. DeCamp also heard various noises, including the sound of a drum, what sounded like someone tap dancing, and even moaning and crying.

Her daughters, Caroline and Kim, told a most unusual story. They shared a bed in the rear bedroom on Christmas Eve, 1985. While Kim read a book and Caroline slept, the bed moved roughly eight inches away from the wall. It was as if someone had picked up the foot of the bed and suddenly pulled it towards the center of the room. Another time Kim came home to find the water running in the bathroom next to the second-floor rear bedroom. When she questioned her mother, who was in the backyard reading the newspaper, Mrs. DeCamp claimed she hadn't been in that bathroom at all that day. Despite all this, Mrs. DeCamp was never afraid during the time her family resided at the haunted house. Mrs. DeCamp is sure that Keefer is a "good spirit."

In 1992, the Ruckarts bought the house. Interestingly, they previously owned a haunted house in Georgia, which was inhabited by the ghost of a young girl. However, neither Alice nor Gordon Ruckart saw or encountered Keefer.

The dwelling, located at 520 Craven Street, is often included in New Bern's Annual Halloween Ghost Walk. The walk is sponsored by the New Bern Historical Society, which also published *Ghost Stories of Old New Bern*. For more information, call the New Bern Historical Society at (252) 638-8558.

POISONOUS

FRUITS

In a storm of emotion, the dishonored wife sank to the ground, sobbing and fighting to catch her breath and control herself. After about an hour she realized what she had to do. Elizabeth stood up, wobbling slightly, and hurried back to the house.

Hilton Head Island, home to Walt Disney's latest resort and family amusement center, is one of South Carolina's most desirable vacation spots, especially for golfers. But before it became a playground for the wealthy, it was a deserted island, a point-of-no-return before entering Georgia. The island was discovered in 1664 by English Sea Captain William Hilton, the island's namesake.

Hilton Head was once an undeveloped terrain of sand dunes and marshland, sprinkled with a few plantation homes and residents. Edmund Thatcher and his wife, Elizabeth, owned one of these homes. Although Elizabeth was said to be a cold woman, she was wildly jealous and possessive of her husband and watched him closely. She noticed his lingering glances at one of their servants, a pretty slave girl named Josephine. Elizabeth began taking long walks, deliberately passing the slave quarters. Soon after she began spying her worst fears were confirmed.

One evening, as the moon hung full and prominent in the

sky, she gasped as she saw her husband's silhouette through a window, caressing this young woman. Despite her suspicions, Elizabeth couldn't believe what she saw. Admittedly, the girl had flawless, light ebony skin, and beauty exuded from her long, lean frame, but still she couldn't believe this was happening to her. She continued staring until the two disappeared from view.

In a storm of emotion, the dishonored wife sank to the ground, sobbing and fighting to catch her breath and control herself. After about an hour she realized what she had to do. Elizabeth stood up, wobbling slightly, and hurried back to the house.

Elizabeth gathered up her jewelry and put it in a small black tote bag. The next day, she took her usual stroll around part of the island, waving to a neighbor, and stopping to examine some interesting shells. As Elizabeth wandered past the slave homes, she pulled the black bag from her cape and slipped into Josephine's room. She dumped out the glimmering jewels in a dresser drawer and then discreetly headed back home.

The couple was entertaining that evening, and over dinner Elizabeth made a great fuss over a guest's gold-and-emerald broach.

"Oh, it's beautiful!" she exclaimed. "I have one very similar, passed on to me by my grandmother. You must see it," she told the woman. She gathered up her skirt and disappeared from the room.

A few minutes later Elizabeth came back, out of breath and very upset.

"They're gone, all gone. My family jewels are missing!" she cried.

After a thorough search, the slaves were questioned. All denied any knowledge of the missing jewelry, so the group proceeded to the slave quarters to look for themselves, and soon found Elizabeth's jewels in Josephine's dresser. When they looked further to see what else she might have taken, they also found a large quantity of poison on her nightstand!

Despite the girl's protests and claims of innocence, Edmund was furious and suspicious that she planned to poison one or both of

*This tree is similar to the one from which
Josephine was hanged.*

them. Josephine was hanged soon after the discovery.

People had begun to forget about the sad story when a courting couple had a romantic picnic under the tree where Josephine died. As the young man was professing his devotion to the girl, a voice was heard softly saying: "No! No! I didn't do it! I didn't do it . . ."

After this, others claimed to hear a sad voice proclaiming the same thing. While some argue it's just the wind, others believe it's the spirit of Josephine, returning to tell listeners of her innocence.

It was later rumored that his wife and the slave girl were not the only women with whom Edmund Thatcher had been keeping company. Another unknown woman may have planted the poison. Or maybe Josephine had been planning to poison her two-timing lover or his callous wife? The truth will never be known.

PRESENCE AT

HAMPTON PLANTATION

She watched as the rocking chair moved. It rocked back and forth as if someone were in it. Muffled noises accompanied the motion, as if someone were softly crying.

The Hampton Plantation, an Adam-style plantation built circa 1730, is an architectural marvel and is steeped in historical significance. Many important patriots and politicians, such as General LaFayette, were entertained in the dining rooms and ballrooms of Hampton. George Washington spent time there during his presidential tour, and Francis Marion used the plantation many times as a retreat during the American Revolution.

For many decades the colonial mansion stood as a rice plantation and then later was used as the private residence of heir Archibald Rutledge, the Poet Laureate of South Carolina, and his wife. Before his death, he asked his relatives if any of them would like to assume responsibility for the house. When none of them expressed any interest, he arranged for it to be sold upon his death to the South Carolina Department of Parks, Tourism, and

Recreation so it could be preserved and so its history could be shared with visitors. Currently the house and its accompanying 322 acres serve as a historic site, museum, and state park.

Hampton Plantation State Park, McClellanville, SC

During its time as a plantation dwelling, it primarily housed three families—the Horrys, the Pinckneys, and the Rutledges. This sad story revolves around the time the Rutledges had possession of the home. The family was extremely well-to-do, and it was expected that each family member would marry someone of equal wealth and prominence.

One of the children, John Henry Rutledge, did not follow those guidelines. Instead, he fell in love with a young woman who was not a "blueblood." Her father was a pharmacist, which in those days was a lower-middle-class profession.

John's domineering mother forbade any union between the two. John went into a deep state of despondency and melancholy. He stayed in his bedroom or sat in a rocking chair in the upstairs library, crying over his lost love. His depression didn't particularly concern or bother his family, for they knew it was best for him not to be with "that girl," and felt in time he would get over his grief.

John didn't get over it and at last went to see the girl's parents. He asked for their help in convincing his family she was right for him, but they refused. Even the young lady's parents were against it, because they didn't feel the marriage could succeed. He then begged the girl to elope with him. She said she couldn't disobey her parents by going against their wishes. She also argued that their parents were probably right and the union was doomed.

John wouldn't give up on his dream. He knew they belonged together. He decided he would give everyone time to realize this. He stayed in a rocking chair in the library or his bedroom for weeks, determined that his mother and the girl would both change their minds. Since John seemed to be taking a long time getting over the girl, his family decided an extended trip might help. They chose Rhode Island, presumably because they had family or friends there. However, their boat had to turn around and return home when John's sister died of yellow fever as he was en route.

Once home, John set out almost immediately for Charleston, where his true love resided. He discovered she had run off and gotten married during his absence. His hope shattered, John hurried back to Hampton Plantation. He entered through the back door where the gun rack was located. Without hesitation, he grabbed a rifle and shot himself. John collapsed at the base of the steps which lead to the upstairs library and bedrooms. The family carried him up to his room and summoned a doctor, but it was too late. John Henry Rutledge died in his bed, within hours of shooting himself.

A couple of weeks after the funeral, a slave was cleaning in the room where the tragedy took place. She watched as the rocking chair where John had spent so much time began rocking. It rocked back and forth as if someone were in it. Muffled noises accompanied the motion, as if someone were softly crying. She stared in dis-

Stairs leading to John Henry Rutledge's room

belief and then screamed. Another servant appeared and witnessed the scene.

For many years, the chair rocked and the moaning continued. Family members and other servants observed it. Many other strange incidents have also been documented at the house. A South Carolina television show, Palmettto Places, did a segment featuring Hampton Plantation. While the crew was setting up, the park attendant on duty told the show's host about the ghost of John Henry Rutledge. Loudly, she proclaimed that was nonsense and that ghosts didn't exist. When it came time to tape the segment, all the lights that had been set up simultaneously burned out, so the taping had to be postponed until replacement lights could be obtained.

The next time the host and her crew attempted to shoot at the former plantation, all the camera batteries died, despite the fact that they had all been charged that morning before leaving the station.

The third time the taping was scheduled, the equipment seemed to be in good working order. The host stood on the front lawn while the crew taped her introduction. Out of the calm air, a whirlwind swept around the host, and only the host. It spun all around her and then dissipated further out in the lawn.

The crew had to return a fourth time to finish taping the segment. When they arrived, the host exited the production van carrying several bouquets of flowers. In response to the park attendant's question of what she was doing with all the flowers, she said she was taking them to John's grave to make peace. She spent some time visiting his tomb and talking to him. Whatever she said must have worked, because nothing unusual happened during the show's taping.

Jayne Ware, a parapsychologist who lives in Winston-Salem, North Carolina, visited Hampton Plantation a few years ago, and she documented the ghost of John Henry Rutledge by taking his photograph.

A couple who toured the house while vacationing in the area mailed a photograph they had taken of the back stairwell. It definitely indicates some kind of presence at the landing of the steps.

I spoke at length with a park attendant on duty, who not only shared this information with me, but also told of bringing his son and nephew to the house late one night. They ventured through the dwelling and up the wooden steps with the aid of a flashlight. The group began hearing noises after only a few minutes. All attest to hearing footsteps and crying. The frightened boys ran out of the house and their father took them home.

All of this information and the images can be found in the "Ghost Log"—ask the attending park ranger to see it. John Henry Rutledge's gravesite can also be seen by those visiting Hampton Plantation. Pay close attention to the wording of the inscription his family chose (because of his suicide) for the tombstone:

In Memory

of

John Henry Rutledge

Son of Frederick and Harriott (Horry) Rutledge

who departed this life

on the 5th of March 1830

aged 21 years

He was distinguished for

Fortitude and firmness

The Goodness and the magnanimity that he

showed even in the agonies of a painful

Death made indelible impressions upon

all who witnessed it

He died in Peace with all men and in the full

Confidence that his Maker would receive

his Soul with that Mercy & Forgiveness

which is the hope & solace of the Penitent

in his approach to the throne of the Eternal

Note: There is a small admission fee for touring Hampton Plantation, which is current-
ly being restored. The mansion is part of Hampton State Park (no admission costs),
which is open year-round with hours varying according to season. It is located fifteen
miles southwest of Georgetown, off US 17. For more information, call (843) 546-9361
or visit their website www.lowcountry-sc.com/hampton.

Crypt of John Henry Rutledge in the Hampton Plantation garden

SEVEN SISTERS

At the end of the month, they collected their pay, packed their bags, and left. They were never heard from again. No one knows what happened to them.

This is one of the most bizarre stories you'll ever hear. It centers around seven sisters. They weren't actual blood sisters, but sisters in fate. Legend has it the seven girls were captured from different African villages and put on a ship to America. They ended up in various households around Nags Head, North Carolina. There they stayed in servitude until the Civil War ended and slaves were freed.

They didn't have nearly enough money to return home. Three of the seven "sisters" wished to remain at Nags Head, where they had been offered jobs by the families who owned them when they had been slaves. The young women wanted to stay until they could earn enough fare for the passage home.

The other four weren't sure if they wanted to go back to Africa and their former lives. They felt they had more opportunities if they stayed in this country, but left Nags Head and started a new life someplace away from where their servitude had taken place. This created a sizable problem, since the sisters had made a promise to each other as they huddled together on the boat. The frightened women swore they'd stay together and always look out for each other. After several lengthy discussions about their futures and what they should do, they came to an unknown agreement.

At the end of the month, they collected their pay, packed their bags, and left. No one heard from them again.

The day after the young women left, a colossal storm created an unimaginable natural phenomenon. Seven hills, nearly the same in size, formed as a result of that strange gale. Commonly known as the "Seven Sisters," the hills were located at Milepost 14, Nags Head, until several years ago when developers destroyed them.

There are as many superstitions involving the sea as there are coastal ghosts. For instance, did you know that thunder, lightning, and fierce winds have been thought to be manifestations of the gods, usually of their anger? If you were struck by lightning or suffered some sort of storm effect, such as being shipwrecked or drowned at sea, it was because the gods were angry with you.

Another sea superstition involves the albatross, which was thought to signify bad wind and foul weather if it circled around a ship in mid-ocean. It was very unlucky to harm an albatross, because it was thought to embody the restless soul of a dead mariner. Some seamen believed this applied to stormy petrels and seagulls, as well.

TREE OF LIFE

The ceremony was attended by the entire village. The chief spoke, musicians played big, round drums, and women chanted in the background, as Running Eagle looked on, numb from head to toe.

*L*egend has it there is a tree of life on Daufuskie Island. A tree that, when combined with the right information, holds the key to life. And, without that knowledge, will inflict a swift death.

This powerful tree was planted many, many years ago by an old Indian chief. He told no one of it save his eldest son. It was special, he explained: "In time, it will produce a berry that is poisonous, but if that same berry is crushed and blended with the right ingredients, has tremendous healing power. I want no one to know about it."

"But, I do not see the harm, father. This tree is a good thing. Our people will be most pleased to learn of its existence."

The wise chief had witnessed human nature for many more years than his offspring. "You must trust me on this, Running Eagle, my son."

The young Indian remained perplexed by his father's wishes, but agreed to honor them. Some years later, the great Indian chief succumbed to old age. His son frequently went to the site of the burgeoning tree, where he had buried his father and felt closer to his spirit. In time he married, and his days were filled with making a life with his new wife. Most of the tribe respected the young Indian, and it was understood that when the prevailing chief died, he would become the next chief of his people. Many of the younger members of the tribe already brought their problems and concerns to Running Eagle.

Daufuskie Island can only be reached by boat, which can be rented or launched from Savannah, Georgia, or Hilton Head, South Carolina. Once on the island, the only vehicles allowed are golf carts, bicycles, and horse-drawn buggies.

One day when he was out hunting, he saw his wife in a clearing several yards away. He dropped everything and ran to her. "What is wrong?" he asked, as his eyes searched hers for an explanation.

"I am with child."

The Indian let out a whoop, picked up his wife, and gently swung her in the air. Everything was fine until the white man began arriving on the island in large numbers.

At first the Indians didn't have a problem with them, but then the settlers began destroying the forest to make homes bigger than they needed. And the men never planted seedlings to replace what they had destroyed. They did not respect the land, and then claimed they didn't have enough food. The settlers made it a habit to come to the Indians whenever their supplies ran low and in exchange offered useless trinkets. Before long, the Indians had had enough. They just wanted to be rid of the white man and have things back the way they were.

There was talk of war. Without usurping the current chief's

authority (who was appointed until Running Eagle was old enough to lead the tribe), Running Eagle gently reminded his people that the island was a big place, and a war would benefit no one. Meanwhile, his wife gave birth to a strong, male baby. The Indian was so proud and happy he thought he might burst. He took the infant to the special tree where he had buried his father and spoke to the newborn of his deceased grandfather.

Soon after this, some of his tribe came down with the deadly fever brought by the white settlers. Running Eagle went to the tree, picked a basket of berries, and concocted the medicine as his father had told him. He fed the medicine to all who were ill, and within twenty-four hours their fever had broken.

The harmony the Indians had struggled to maintain was soon shattered when two Indians were accidentally killed by a white man who was hunting on the Indians' side of the island. The Indians would not believe it was an accident. The tribe believed the white man was trying to get rid of the Indians and take their land. Even Running Eagle's temper was high, since one of the Indians killed had been his brother. And, he felt that even if it had been a mistake, the white man was starting to hunt and fish more and more on the Indians' side of the island, depleting their resources. Still, he didn't believe war would be the best solution, particularly since the white colonists had guns.

Incidents continued, and finally Running Eagle felt he had no choice but to take action. He picked a big basket of berries from the secret tree and took it to the white settlers as a peace offering. Of course, the poisonous berries killed the settlers who ate more than a few. The settlers realized what must have happened and set out to find the tree bearing the poisonous fruits. After they chopped down the massive tree, they began preparing for battle with the Indians.

The Indians were no match for the settlers, and the braves were driven back to their village. Showing no mercy, the settlers followed them and continued to attack. They shot relentlessly. Some of the shots missed the warring Indians and instead hit women and children. Running Eagle's wife and baby were injured when a stray bullet hit the child and then passed through his body to his mother's as she was holding him.

The Indian ran like the wind across the forest and high up the bluffs where the tree was hidden. He knew he had to hurry and get the medicine back to his family and the many who lay injured and dying. When he finally arrived at the site of the tree, the Indian cried out in shock. There was nothing left of it but a stump and a couple of scattered berries.

Running Eagle was forced to watch his family and friends die. There was nothing that could be done for them but to stop the bleeding and pray. His prayers went unanswered, for his wife and son died along with many of his tribe. He now understood what his father had tried to tell him. He had misused the tree's gift, and now he paid a heavy price for it.

The Indian planted another tree, this one without berries, and buried his wife and son at its base. The ceremony was attended by the entire village. The chief spoke; musicians played loud, round drums; and women chanted in the background as a numb Running Eagle looked on.

The memorial tree grew to be the biggest tree on Daufuskie Island. Early residents allegedly heard the sound of drums, occasionally. And, if they looked up to the bluffs, they thought they saw an Indian squatting by the tree, as if visiting his family.

The Indians have been gone from the island for too many years to count, but the battle on Bloody Point will never be forgotten. Translated into English, Daufuskie means "place of blood," a fitting name for the island, considering its history.

The entire island of Daufuskie is on the National Register of Historic Places. When English settlers tried to establish a colony on Daufuskie, the Indians attempted to stop them. As a result, two famous Indian battles took place on the island. The first massacre was initiated by the Indians, who attacked a scout boat from Beaufort. The second attack, a larger one known as the Yemassee Indian War of 1715, occurred when settlers ambushed a group of Indians on the southeastern tip of the island. All the Indians died during this battle except one, who swam to Tybee Island, in Georgia. Hence, the name for that part of the island is Bloody Point.

BURIED

TREASURE

"If anyone tries to dig up my riches, they will have to get past me, alive or dead," he threatened. And with that, the pirates got ready for battle."

"Aye, what a glorious booty!" the pirate exclaimed. The buccaneer and his band of pirates had just successfully seized a Spanish galleon's cargo, including gold and silver, jeweled religious icons, silks and fine linens, muskets, and two kegs of gunpowder.

They landed at a stretch of beach near Charleston, to hide out and celebrate as only those who have endured life at sea can. As the merrymaking grew in intensity, one of the crew ran to the captain and told him he had spotted a military ship on the horizon.

Knowing that this meant the U.S. Navy had found them and was on the way to capture them and recover the treasure, the captain had it hidden.

"If anyone tries to dig up my riches, they will have to get past me, alive or dead!" he threatened. And with that, the pirates got ready for battle.

The sea robbers fought the good fight, but were ill prepared for such a confrontation. They were outmanned and outmaneuvered. The captain was killed, along with the rest of the small group of tired, drunken pirates. The crew of the navy vessel searched the island and the marauder's ship but couldn't find the loot. They spent several days excavating the surrounding tract of coastal ground, but short of digging up the entire island, determined it would be impossible to find the hiding spot. The officers finally gave up and called off the search.

The story circulated that there was buried treasure at Charleston's Morrison Island, now known as Folly Beach, and that it belonged to anyone who could find it. Treasure hunters soon filled the island, shoveling up sand, dirt, bushes, and trees in hopes of finding a fortune. Not one of these men, women, or children came close to the burial spot.

After the initial frenzied efforts turned up nothing more than debris and junk, people began to believe that the pirate never buried any "booty" on Morrison Island. Attempts to discover the treasure became few and far between. However, a group of soldiers stationed at nearby Ft. Moultrie decided to try. As the men inadvertently came close to the treasure, they saw an immense man in pirate garb standing with his hands on his hips and a shimmering silver sword at his side. Before they could talk it over and figure out what to make of it, or what to do, one of the men advanced towards the figure. A freak earthquake, the only one of any consequence to ever hit the Charleston area, occurred at that moment and took the man's life. The others left, terrified, believing the menacing-looking pirate had appeared to warn them to stay away. They swore they'd never step foot on the island again.

Others have tried to take the treasure, but they also claimed to see the dead buccaneer. They had heard the sight of him was a final warning, and they wisely took it as such and left.

Another group of determined men tried to find the fortune. As they came ashore, they noticed the darkening skies and the sea starting to get rough, but dismissed it as their greed for the gold outweighed their common sense. After a couple of hours of looking, the men accidentally neared the spot. There stood a massive figure grasping a long, gleaming blade pointed in their direction.

Some of the men started back to the boat, while the others continued towards the figure. The foreboding pirate raised his cutlass as they closed in on him. The rest of the men suddenly turned on their heels and ran to the boat to catch up with the others, anxious to get away. Despite the high and extremely rough swells created by the violent storm that embraced the island, the men pushed the boat into the water and jumped in.

The first man to flee after witnessing the pirate was found the next day, clinging to the side of the boat. None of the other men were ever seen again. To this day, no one claims to have excavated the treasure that the dead pirate captain so closely guards.

Note: This story has often been told with the identity of the buccaneer being Blackbeard or Captain Kidd. However, neither of these sea robbers died in a battle around the Charleston area.

CROSSING THE

DRAWBRIDGE

The parties were reminiscent of those held by F. Scott Fitzgerald's "great" Jay Gatsby. Servants, numbering almost as many as the guests, circulated continuously with trays laden with champagne and fancy hors d'oeuvres.

Just before crossing the bridge into Wrightsville Beach, there is an exclusive, gated golf community called Landfall. Before it existed, much of that land was the site of only one estate. A meticulously groomed, expansive lawn and surrounding wooded area complimented the impressive, enormous manor. Belonging to a wealthy industrialist, Pembroke Jones Sr., the mansion was often full of entrepreneurs, politicians, and celebrities such as the Cornings and the Rockefellers.

The parties were reminiscent of those held by F. Scott Fitzgerald's "great" Jay Gatsby. Servants, numbering almost as many as the guests, circulated continuously with trays laden with champagne and fancy hors d'oeuvres. Instructions were given that no guest should have a glass less than half full or should want for anything. Sparing no expense, Mr. Jones hired a multitude of musicians , and it is even said that he had exotic animals as entertainment. Guests could sip cocktails while mingling in the immense foyer or sit at one of the many tables set up in the formal gardens. The terrace served as an alcove for the band, and a series of tables boasting a lavish buffet were set up only yards away.

The host's son, Pembroke Jr., always attended these opulent functions, usually with a girl on each arm. This particular night, though, the son's attention was fixed on one of the servants. The petite, dark-haired girl who wore her long hair up in a wide, red bow was the daughter of a fisherman from Sea Gate. While the young man enjoyed himself all evening, he couldn't keep his mind off the girl distributing flutes of champagne.

When the party ended, he took his date to her house and promptly returned home. The servants had just finished cleaning up and were headed home. He asked the girl if she would like a ride home. She smiled shyly and nodded yes.

No one knows what happened after the young girl left with Pembroke Jones Jr. The girl was found dead on Shell Road, not far from her house. The boy claimed to have taken her directly home but did not see her inside, as she had asked him not to. An investigation revealed the girl had recently broken up with her boyfriend, whose whereabouts that night were unknown. Since Pembroke's father was so affluent and influential, combined with the small possibility that the boyfriend could be guilty, no charges were filed against the young man. Although he wasn't arrested, it was commonly believed he did try to force his attentions on the girl, and she either died falling out of the vehicle trying to escape, or the boy was so infuriated when she declined his affection that he killed her in a fit of rage.

A girl has been seen many times by many people near the drawbridge on Airlie Road, formerly Shell Road. Witnesses report the girl is small in size, with brown hair spilling out of a loosely tied red bow. The girl's clothes are soiled, and she appears to be crying. Whenever anyone turns around to go back and help the distressed young lady, she vanishes.

Fathers forbade their daughters from seeing Pembroke. The young man was an outcast, invited to social functions only because no one wanted to alienate the rich Pembroke Jones Sr. His peers did not mix with him, and some even openly sneered at him.

Ironically, his vehicle was found overturned one night, with the dead boy sprawled next to it. His father cried foul play, but local authorities, who could find no evidence supporting this accusation, thought alcohol was to blame. Since the boy took to drinking heavily once he was ostracized by the community, and a bottle of whiskey was found near the corpse, it seemed a reasonable explanation.

Could it be that maybe he saw the ghost of the girl, and the vision spooked him so much that he wrecked his car and died?

After Pembroke Sr. died, the Jones estate was abandoned and fell into a state of disrepair. The two giant lion statues that stood at the entrance to the house were defaced, and the house was eventually destroyed in an accidental fire caused by vagrants.

More recently, ghost seekers looking to catch a glimpse of the Airlie Ghost have sometimes been a problem for the owners of Airlie Gardens, located near the area of many of the ghost's sightings.

She is still seen on occasion.

An article written by Jefferson C. Weaver for *Carolina Style* magazine details his firsthand sighting of the Airlie Ghost. He claimed to see the ghost at 2:42 A.M. Weaver said, "She stepped out from [behind] the trunk of one of the trees on the north side of the road—a chestnut-haired young woman in a formal, mid-calf, yet faintly old-fashioned dress." And then she was gone. When he notified the sheriff's department he learned that reports such as his were fairly common.

WHIMSICAL

HARPIST

Unfortunately, the captain discovered they were all too poor to pay for their tickets, and once he found out he put them out at the first port he could.

Southport is a quaint waterfront town near Fort Fisher and Bald Head Island. The entire town's population is a mere 2,400. There isn't much to see or do there, with the exception of a movie occasionally being filmed in the former fishing community. Its quiet streets are narrow, lined with big beautiful trees and stately old buildings and houses.

At one time the town's centerpiece was the Brunswick Inn. The waterfront bed and breakfast was so big it was equivalent to several blocks. But now all that remains is a large, two-story whitewashed structure. Guests usually stop off on their way to one of North Carolina's myriad coastal resorts. Their visits consist of only a night or two.

One guest, however, has stayed for over a century, ringing up quite a large bill. It doesn't seem likely anyone will ever be able to collect, since he is a ghost.

He is the straggling spirit of Tony Caseletta, an Italian immigrant-musician who fled from New York City in 1882. Caseletta left town with two other musicians who were equally broke and unhappy with their situations. The trio booked passage on a steamer headed south. The men didn't know where they would end up, or even where they wanted to end up, only that they wanted out of the hard, cold winter climate of the northern United States.

The musicians thoroughly enjoyed the cruise and often entertained other guests with the pleasing sounds of the trio's harp, cello, and mandolin. Unfortunately, once the captain discovered they were all too poor to pay for their tickets, he put them out at the first port he could. The resourceful group found their way to the small, friendly community of Southport and knew they had discovered their new home. They begged the proprietor of the Brunswick Inn to let them stay, at least temporarily, in exchange for entertaining guests and helping out around the inn.

Since the owner did need a hand with the large inn, and the musicians were very good, he agreed. Pretty soon, residents from all over the county were hiring the men to play at various functions. The three happily lived in seaside Southport, earning a living doing what they loved.

One day, they attempted to learn how to sail by borrowing a small craft and heading towards Bald Head Island. Since none of the young men were familiar with boats or sailing techniques, it's not surprising the boat capsized less than halfway to the island. The trio were thrown from the small vessel when it flipped over, and Tony's head hit the bow. Before the other men could save him, he drowned. Tony Casseletta was buried at Smithville Burial Ground.

A concert was scheduled the night of Tony's funeral, but Tony's friends honored their agreement by performing as planned. In memory of their friend, they set up his harp between their chairs. The unmanned harp emitted music as if it were being played! Since that time, former guests at Brunswick say they have heard the soft sounds of a string instrument, possibly a harp.

The inn is now a private residence, owned and occupied by

The old Brunswick Inn, on 301 East Bay Street in Southport, NC, is a private residence that is home to the ghost of Tony Caseletta.

Barry and Mary Collari, as well as Mary's widowed mother, Alice Arrington. While Barry Collari and Alice Arrington haven't heard anything, Mary says that on a couple of occasions she has heard sounds that could be from a harp.

WEEPING ARCH

Funeral processions must enter and exit the cemetery by passing under the imposing gate. For nearly a century and a half, people who visit Cedar Grove have told of feeling drops of liquid hit them as they cross through the entrance.

T he epidemic spread through New Bern at an alarming rate. Most of the men, women, and children it struck succumbed quickly to the deadly yellow fever. While the disease, transmitted by infected mosquitoes, is still a threat in many parts of the world, it is no longer a problem in the United States. In earlier times, especially in coastal areas and particularly in the summertime, yellow fever disease presented a serious danger. Many wealthy families packed up and left during summer and then returned in the fall when mosquitoes were less prevalent, and the threat of catching yellow fever was considerably diminished.

But some argue the epidemic of 1798 originated from one of the many ships that harbored at the port city. In those days, passengers and crew often contracted yellow fever while on board.

Whether the disease was brought by ship or manifested within the city, the important thing was the number of lives it claimed. At first the bodies were buried behind New Bern's Christ Church. However, the small churchyard wasn't nearly big enough to hold all the deceased, so a separate cemetery, Cedar Grove, was established. Cedar Grove Cemetery is denoted by a distinctive entrance gate, added in 1854. The stately, triple-arch gateway is comprised of marl and coquina rock.

Funeral processions must enter and exit the cemetery by passing under the imposing gate. For nearly a century and a half, people who visit Cedar Grove have told of feeling drops of liquid hit them as they cross through the entrance. That seemingly odd occurrence is actually easily explained. Rainwater is temporarily cisterned in the porous shell rock, where it slowly drips down until all the water has leaked out.

What cannot be reasoned away is that raindrops pelt mourners even when there hasn't been precipitation for weeks! And, it is inexplicable how those drops often have a reddish color that can be seen when they touch the skin or ground, but the drops never stain clothing.

Careful examination of the gate has never revealed any answers to these perplexing questions. Perhaps it doesn't matter, except to those who are pelted by the drops as they hurry through the weeping arch, for they are the ones who will next visit the cemetery in their final slumber as a "guest of honor," according to legend.

Cedar Grove Cemetery and its marvelous three-part gate still exist today. It is located just past the historic district of New Bern, at the junction of Queen and George Streets.

 The sound of church bells was once widely believed to drive away demons, both those brought by tropical storms and hurricanes, and those who flitted about the world seeking to harm the souls and bodies of men.

SUNSET LODGE

Revered by local businessmen, he was asked to help with the "Bordello Project." Soon thereafter, he met an attractive young woman. She had a certain look and style that was clearly recognizable to anyone. And, she had enough attitude to keep anyone in line.

International Paper decided to make Georgetown, South Carolina, their corporate headquarters. The company began building their enormous plant in 1936, promising that when it was finished it would create much-needed jobs for the town's residents. However, such a large facility required many men and quite a long time to complete. After a few complaints from some of Georgetown's female citizens, it was decided it would be in the town's best interest to provide amusement for the many imported workers. Ultimately, a bordello was considered the best solution to keep the men out of trouble.

Wealthy businessman and Boston Red Sox owner, Tom Yawkey, spent every winter at his home on nearby South Island. Revered by local businessmen, he was asked to help with the "Bordello Project." Soon thereafter, he met an attractive young woman. She had a certain look and style that was clearly recognizable to anyone. And, she had enough attitude to keep anyone in line. Yawkey knew instantly she would be perfect to run the brothel. He carefully approached the woman with his business proposition, and after further discussions, she agreed.

The perfect property was found, outside the town limits, of course, and ladies who were healthy, attractive, and had enough etiquette to border on classy were selected. Most came from surrounding municipalities and were anxious to make some real money and lead a more interesting life. That they did! The young ladies moved into apartments, erected in back of the two-story house where the Madame resided, which became known as Sunset Lodge.

It was understood the young ladies were free to buy any supplies or luxuries they desired from Georgetown, but they weren't to frequent the city proper. That was all right with the Madame, as she loved the comfort and quiet of the stately old house. She had made the house a real home by decorating it with many fine antiques and objets d'art. One of her favorite pieces was an oversized mirror, which was gilded with gold around the scalloped edges of the frame. The Madame also took great pleasure in gardening, and many vibrantly colored flowers and blooming bushes surrounded the house. Having grown up in a big, noisy northern city, she embraced the isolation and subdued beauty of the area. Orders were placed over the phone and deliveries made to the bordello; shopkeepers often hand-delivered the items just for a chance to visit with Madame or her girls.

The reputation of Sunset Lodge became well known, and men from all ages and occupations visited the women. Sea captains, merchants, doctors, salesmen, and even politicians enjoyed the company of the women of Sunset Lodge.

It is rumored that Tom Yawkey even brought business associates and friends to the brothel. Some took the girls out on their yachts for lengthy cruises to tropical places. A taxi service was established to take the girls to the airport or bring clients to the bordello.

It seemed many enjoyed Sunset Lodge, and it was great for Georgetown merchants. The girls bought many items, and customers also purchased little gifts for them. But, in 1969, the sheriff shut down the brothel without warning. He said it was illegal, and he couldn't look the other way any longer. No one ever discovered what really prompted his action. It may have been that the wife of a politician or local businessman tired of her husband's extramarital activities. Whatever the reason, the girls were forced to leave in a hurry, except the Madame, who refused to leave her beloved home. Since she was old by this time, no one saw the harm.

She stayed in the house until her death, when it was sold, furnished. The new owners said her spirit was still present. The couple would often hear the door to her old bedroom open and close without explanation. Many felt it was her spirit keeping an eye on her cherished home.

After a while, the new residents decided it was time to do some redecorating, and they were standing in front of the massive mirror left by the Madame. It was not only the first item she had brought into Sunset Lodge, but also one of her very favorite pieces.

It was a beautiful mirror and certainly an antique of value, but the couple wasn't sure it fit in with their new decor. While they were trying to decide if they should keep it or take it down, the mirror fell to the floor. Upon examination, the couple found nothing more than a small scratch on the upper right corner, where it had taken most of the impact of the fall. No reason could be found for its coming off the wall after all the years it had hung there. As they knelt over the mirror, the couple saw something they couldn't believe. For a split second, a reflection of a woman wearing a long, fancy dress was seen in the mirror.

Without further discussion, they put the mirror back in the same spot it had occupied since the dwelling became Sunset Lodge and never again considered removing the Madame's favorite piece.

Sadly, in 1992, Sunset Lodge caught fire and burned to the

ground. An RV park and some run-down apartments now exist at the site of the old brothel, and the only indication there was such a place is an old brick sign that reads SUNSET LODGE.

*The sign is all that remains of Sunset Lodge and its apartments.
It is nine miles south of Georgetown, SC.*

LOST COLONY

Nothing was going as planned. They had not gotten essential supplies in Haiti, as scheduled, and the nearby Indians had proven to be less than happy to share their land with the white man. In fact, they had already attacked the first expedition.

Sir Walter Raleigh, soldier, seaman, and explorer, was the driving force behind the push to establish civilization in the New World. In 1587, Raleigh's dream came true. He was granted permission by Queen Elizabeth I to set up a colony in America, where each settler would be given five hundred acres. It was to be at Chesapeake Bay, Virginia, where there was a good harbor and reportedly friendly Indians. John White, part of this brave group of adventurers, was delegated governor of this new settlement, and twelve of the men in the group were designated his assistants.

That year, three ships set sail from Plymouth, England, to deliver the courageous assembly of 117 men, women, and children to their new homeland. The ships were to anchor briefly at Roanoke Island, North Carolina, to bring supplies to an expedition already in America before continuing on to their final destination. After two hard months at sea, the crew spotted the island,

and after anchoring, the occupants of the boat hastily disembarked for their first glimpse of this New World.

As the group looked around in awe and trepidation at their remote and primitive surroundings, Captain Fernandez gave them incredible news. He informed everyone that they could go no farther north. Since summer was nearly over, he would not risk the lives of his crew or of the colonists by attempting to reach Chesapeake. The captain gave them what provisions he could and then left the small, unprepared band of pilgrims on the island to fend for themselves until spring of the following year, when Fernandez promised to return for them.

Nothing was going as planned. They had not gotten essential supplies in Haiti, as scheduled, and the nearby Indians had proven to be less than happy to share their land with the white man. In fact, they had already attacked the first expedition.

Manteo, a judicious Indian Chief, had been asked by the English to help keep the peace. He was considered "Lord of Roanoke" by the English who had met him. Chief Manteo and Governor White respected each other and got along very well. The pair worked hard to make peace between the disgruntled Indians and settlers. They arranged a meeting between some of the leaders of the Indian tribes and the settlers in hopes of diffusing the increasing problems between the two groups.

Confusion over the actual date of the meeting caused even more of a rift. When the Indians didn't show up on the day the settlers thought they were supposed to, the white men took it as an overt sign of hostility and a total lack of willingness to try to work things out. The colonists subsequently attacked an Indian village, killing one Indian and wounding others. From then on, it was only a matter of time before another skirmish took place.

Meanwhile, Governor John White's daughter gave birth to an angelic-looking baby girl. Christened Virginia Dare, the tiny infant had no idea what a big deal her birth was, for she was the first child born in the New World. The newborn was also a source of great fascination to the Indians, who had never seen such delicate ivory skin and intense blue eyes.

Immediately after that, Governor White was forced to go back to England for supplies if the colonists were to survive. He took the ship belonging to the first expedition and headed for England. When he arrived, the ship was ordered into service for the Queen to aid in the war between the English and Spanish. The timing couldn't be worse. White petitioned the Queen through Sir Walter Raleigh to be allowed to take supplies back to America. But it was nearly three years before he was able to get passage on a vessel traveling anywhere near Roanoke Island.

When John White and the other privateers arrived at Roanoke Island, there were no colonists. A protracted search revealed nothing that could give them a clue as to what had happened to the 117 pilgrims. They found a suit of armor on the sandy shore, and its rusted condition indicated it had been there were quite awhile. Strangely, the houses had all been taken down, and a fortification put up. On one of its outside posts was carved "Croatoan," the name of a nearby island. A tree near the water had what appeared to be a hastily carved "CRO." It seemed someone had paused just long enough to start etching the word "Croatoan," but had either been stopped abruptly by lack of time or by something more sinister.

The settlers had agreed if they had to abandon Roanoke, they would leave word of their destination by carving it on a tree trunk. A Maltese Cross, the prearranged signal indicating they were forcibly being made to leave, was supposed to accompany it. No cross was found carved on any surface. So, it is not clear whether they were run off by Indians or had to relocate to find food.

White was ready to travel to Croatoan to look for the group, but the other privateers convinced him they didn't have enough food and equipment for such a trip. Truth be known, the pirates didn't really want to be distracted any longer looking for some missing settlers. They were anxious to get back to their prosperous activities. White was forced to go on with the group, but did get word to Sir Walter Raleigh, who continued searching for the colonists until 1602. He never found so much as a trace of them.

Some say they were attacked and killed by the Indians, and their bones were worn as necklaces and other ornamentation. Others insist the men were killed, while the women and children were taken into various tribes. Virginia Dare was reportedly made an Indian princess, worshipped by an entire tribe. Still others believe some of the colonists escaped, but ended up somewhere other than Croatoan or its surrounding area. Whatever really happened, one thing seems certain. Their fate will remain a mystery.

Fort Raleigh is now a 150-acre National Historic Site. Visitors are welcome to explore the reconstructed fort. And, a visitors' center holds artifacts, replicas, exhibits, and a short film detailing the life of those early settlers.

A spectacular outdoor drama highlighting the story of the Lost Colony takes place each summer evening. Lost Colony, considered the grandfather of all outdoor shows, debuted in 1937. For more information about the drama, call (252) 473-2127 or (800) 488-5012 or visit their website www.thelostcolony.org.

The Lost Colony story immortalized on stage.
(Courtesy of The Lost Colony Outdoor Drama, Manteo, NC)

The Squatter

Bogue Sound, in North Carolina, is comprised of islands created in the late 1930s when the U.S. Army Corps of Engineers dug the Intracoastal Waterway, a protected channel for commercial and pleasure craft traveling up and down the East Coast. To make the waterway, the Army Corps of Engineers dredged millions of tons of sand from the bottoms of sounds, creeks, and rivers, and then deposited it in piles, out of the way. As the water drained, the sand settled, creating islands that are called cut banks. Some of these banks are large and appear on navigational charts.

According to some folks, there is a white-haired man with a silvery beard who lives on one of these otherwise-deserted isles. The sixty-something squatter has a hut on the beach. Reportedly, his wife died young, but he has grown children, as well as a brother who lives somewhere in Virginia.

The few people who claim to have seen or met the man either cannot recall on which of the numerous islands he resides, or refuse to disclose the location so that no one will bother him. If he is real, what does he do when nor'easters and hurricanes blow through? And what drove him to cut himself off from the rest of the world and live in a hovel on a deserted island in Bogue Sound?

Note: The Squatter is not to be confused with The Hermit of Fort Fisher.

ABANDONED

BRIDE

The girl was so upset that she turned and ran off. Once out of sight, she stopped along the water's edge to catch her breath. She teetered, unaccustomed to the heels she was wearing, and fell in. The weight of the dress prevented her from being able to swim or pull herself out of the water.

The two met secretly whenever he was in port. They had to, since she was promised to another man. The girl's parents had arranged for her to marry a man from a prominent family and had no idea her heart belonged to another. It wouldn't have mattered anyway, since her beloved was a young sailor from a poor family. They both knew they had no future, but carried on seeing each other until her parents finalized the wedding and the date was announced. Although she knew the day would come, it tugged cruelly at her heart that she would never again see the sailor or listen to him talk about his dream of one day owning his own ship.

On her wedding day, she got word his boat was docking. Garbed in her bridal attire, she ran to the harbor to see the young man one last time, hoping for a miracle. What she saw broke her heart. He was coming up the walkway arm in arm with another woman! They were laughing and carrying on as if no one were around.

The girl was so upset that she turned and ran off. Once out of sight, she stopped along the water's edge to catch her breath. She teetered, unaccustomed to the heels she was wearing, and fell in. The weight of the dress prevented her from being able to swim or pull herself out of the water. Her soaked veil clung around her neck like a noose, and the poor girl nearly drowned.

Her brother, who had been sent to find her as it was nearly time for the ceremony, happened upon her. He rescued her and then asked what she was doing. "Had she taken leave of her senses?" he thought.

Hysterical by now, his sister told of the sailor and everything that had happened. The enraged brother vowed revenge for the unfair advantage the mariner had taken of his little sister. Before she could stop him, he took off. When he found the sailor he fatally shot him.

The wedding was called off by the groom-to-be after hearing of the scandal. Nearly a week later, a young woman came to see the abandoned bride. The broken-hearted girl recognized her as the woman who was with her true love on the docks that terrible day her world fell apart.

"I know you probably do not wish to see me, but if you will hear me out I will go, and you'll never see me again."

The woman proceeded to tell the abandoned bride she had been asked by the sailor to be at the harbor that day. He was sure the bride would be there to meet his boat and to ask if there was any way they could be together before she made a lifelong commitment to another. He had revealed he loved the girl very much and was afraid he wouldn't have the strength to let her go; the sailor felt the price for them to be together was too high. She would have to forsake her family, live a lifestyle far less grand than what she was accustomed to, and spend a great deal of time alone, as he was away at sea frequently. She had hinted on more than one occasion that she was willing to do so, but he couldn't bear the thought of her giving up so much just to be with him. He thought of a plan to make it look like he didn't care, like she was just another girl he amused himself with, so she would go ahead and get married and have the life she deserved.

"Why should I believe this?" the distraught girl cried out.

"Because I am . . . was, his sister."

The news devastated the young girl. She went crazy. Her bouts of insanity included putting on her wedding dress and standing at the door, awaiting the arrival of the dead man's ship. She would talk to herself, muttering that when he arrived they'd have to leave immediately to make it to the church in time for the ceremony. Sometimes she worked herself up so much that in order to calm her down, her brother would put on clothes such as those worn by a seaman and walk her down to the harbor to "wait for the groom's ship."

For years people claimed they had seen a young lady in a wedding gown strolling around the docks of Beaufort with a young man wearing a sailor's outfit.

Horses'

HOOVES

On Halloween night of 1986, a "ghost watch" was arranged. It was not open to the public, only to an intimate group of twenty. A séance was held at midnight, but none of the participants ever revealed what occurred that night.

*P*oplar Grove was a huge 628-acre produce plantation. The thriving plantation stood until 1849, when the original manor house was destroyed by fire. The estate was rebuilt the following year by Joseph Mumford Foy and continued to serve as a prosperous plantation until the Civil War. During the Civil War, Union armies took over the house and used it as a base until the war ended. After that, lucrative peanut crops became the plantation's primary harvest.

Poplar Grove remained a critical part of the community and local economy until the Foy family sold it to the Poplar Grove Foundation, which was formed in 1971 to maintain the historic estate. In 1980, the plantation's doors were opened to the public. It is at that point the ghost was discovered.

The ghost is commonly known as Nora Frazier Foy, who lived in the manor house from 1850 until her death in 1923. Known as "Aunt Nora," the ghost has never done any harm, but she cer-

The Poplar Grove Plantation, nine miles north of Wilmington, NC.

tainly makes her presence known in many ways.

Staff at the on-site restaurant, which was added when the estate became a museum, claim the ghost must be to blame for at least some of the unexplainable events that have taken place over the years. They tell of hearing music, but not being able to find its source. The staff also report toilets flushing by themselves. And, often managers would turn the lights off when locking up for the night only to watch them come back on again! One manager swears someone kept picking up the phone while she was on it, but she was the only person in the building at the time. Another manager was in the office one night working late and watched as the pages of a nearby notepad started to slowly flip through all the sheets. Frightened, she left the room and ran into one of the cooks, who also was spooked by a peculiar occurrence. As he was finishing up for the night, the startled man witnessed all the pots and pans in the kitchen come off the wall hooks and simultaneously crash to the floor!

However, these incidents pale in comparison to one that happened outside. One night as a patron was walking to his car, located in the nearby gravel parking lot, he heard a noise. It was unmistakably the sound of galloping horses' hooves. When he looked up, he saw a carriage led by two broad, white horses. It was headed down the tree-lined road of the estate. The carriage contained two people: a man in a tuxedo and a woman wearing a formal gown. The clothes didn't look contemporary, but rather like what would have been worn many decades ago when the plantation hosted dance parties. The man continued staring, almost in a stupor, as the fancy, horse-drawn buggy disappeared from view. Realizing the absurdity of it, he jumped into his car and followed the carriage, determined to find out what was going on.

He never caught up with the couple in the carriage. Knowing they couldn't have gotten far, he doubled back and drove all around the area, but never found any sign of them, except for some imprints of horses' hooves on the unpaved road.

On Halloween night of 1986, Ann Marley, director of cultural arts programs for Poplar Grove, set up a "ghost watch." It was not open to the public, only to an intimate group of twenty. A séance was held at midnight, but neither Ann Marley nor the other participants ever revealed what occurred that night. Maybe you can get her to tell you. . . . Or, find out for yourself at the annual Halloween Haunted Barn and Trail Festival.

Poplar Grove Historic Plantation is open to the public most of the year. The plantation is nine miles north of Wilmington, off Highway 17. Call (910) 686-9989 for more information or visit their website www.poplargrove.com.

${\mathscr{B}}$ LAZING FURY

She leaned over and kissed him on the cheek. And with that she walked out of the bar and out of his dreams. Sagging against the great piano, the man felt bitter pain like he had never known.

T here once was a saloon in Beaufort, unlike any establishment that preceded it or has been built since. The saloon was constructed to accommodate the many seafaring men that docked at the adjacent harbor. The tavern had everything these men could want.

Lively music played every night, thanks to the efforts of a skillful piano player. A minimum of six hostesses were on hand at all times to entertain the patrons. The savory smell of steaks sizzling in the kitchen lured men almost before their vessels had properly docked. And, for the devoted gambler, a card game could usually be found somewhere in the enormous structure.

The saloon was a two-story building, roughly the size of a

warehouse. The main level contained the kitchen, dance hall, a bar equipped with stools and tables of varied sizes, and a big, ebony piano. The upper level contained rooms men could rent so that they could take a bath, store their belongings, or have some privacy for a while. The bartender was provided with room and board, so he had a bedroom upstairs. Food and liquor supplies were locked in a storage room.

The nights frequently ended in a brawl between seamen, due to a combination of liquor and rowdy dispositions. One night, a young man shot another man who had accused him of cheating at cards. It was only in the arm, but no one ever charged the zealous player of cheating again. Sometimes the hostesses had to call on the bartender or piano player to deal with an overly friendly patron. However, the musician and bartender kept a close eye on the young ladies, trying to anticipate trouble and prevent it from occurring.

The piano player grew extremely protective of one of the girls in particular. Every time he saw her dancing or talking with one of the patrons, a ball of jealousy grew within him. He began to intercede when it wasn't necessary, because he couldn't stand to see anyone flirting with the girl. One night, he felt a burly young man was forcing too much of his attention on the girl, and he told the man so. Laughingly, the man pushed him backwards and continued dancing with the young lady. The musician made another effort, but the mariner knocked him down with just one swift punch. The girl bent down to check on him; upon realizing he was all right, she told him to leave her alone.

"You've got to stop doing this. You're going to get us both fired," she pleaded.

From then on he came to hate the smoke-filled saloon. If only they didn't work there, they could be together, he imagined. His dream girl wouldn't have to put up with the offensive men who frequented the bar. The idea had such appeal to him that he thought about it all the time. From his obsessing, he came up with a plan and couldn't wait to share it with the girl.

One night, as they were cleaning and closing up, he nervously began playing a slow, melodious song. As he played, she continued to sweep, seemingly unaffected by his music. After he finished, the girl still said nothing, so the musician approached her and asked what she had thought of the tune.

"It was nice."

"I was hoping you would like it. I wrote it. It's what plays in my head and my heart every time I'm around you," he confessed. "I . . . I . . . I'm in love with you!" he bravely stammered.

The girl looked up at him as she was clearing the tables and smiled. "You can't be. You don't even know me." Seeing his unwavering stare filled with hope and devotion, the hostess continued. "Look, I'm going to be honest with you, which is more than a man's ever been to me. You're a nice guy. I like working with you. I even like most of your music. But, I'm sort of seeing the bartender."

The bartender! Sensing his dream was slipping away, he made a final desperate effort. "We can leave this place. I can make a decent living somewhere else playing my music. You wouldn't have to work in a place like this," the piano player exclaimed breathlessly.

"I like my job. I like dancing every night, flirting, and getting paid for it. Sure, sometimes the men get carried away, but I can handle that. I definitely like the money. I could never earn this kind of money working in a shop or something. I even like the smell of this smoky, musty saloon. I couldn't live like you're talking. Never."

She leaned over and kissed him on the cheek. And with that she walked out of the bar and out of his dreams. Sagging against the great piano, the lovesick man felt bitter pain and anger like he had never known. He clutched the purse she had inadvertently left behind. It smelled of her perfume. The musician snapped. Without thinking, he ran home, got what he needed, and returned. Within minutes he had set fire to the saloon.

As he watched it burn, the flames shooting higher and faster, he began to feel better. Without the bartender or saloon, she was bound to change her mind. Then he spotted the girl in an upstairs window. She couldn't get the window open, and apparently she was unable or afraid to smash it and jump, so she was stuck inside the burning building.

What was she doing inside? Had she come back for her purse? Or to see the bartender? Maybe even to tell him she had changed her mind? During the few seconds he was pondering this, the bartender appeared at his side. He quickly told the astonished musician he had been in his room and smelled smoke. When he opened his door and saw fire ripping through the structure, he quickly leaped out his window and into the bushes below.

The old wooden establishment had gone up in flames like a pile of kindling in a fireplace and was now out of control.

"We've got to do something! " he cried out.

"There's nothing we can do. The saloon is about to burn to the ground. It would be suicide to try to enter it now," the bartender answered.

The musician, knowing he was to blame, threw his coat around himself and ran inside the blazing building. He never made it out, nor did the girl.

People started hearing music the night following this tragedy. It was always the same melancholy piano tune, but its source has never been discovered. The song often mystically floated through the air without any apparent origin.

MISS MARY AND

THE MARINES

Miss Mary, as she is affectionately known, wears a nineteenth century-style, long-sleeved calico dress. The white-haired, elderly woman has spooked many a Marine stationed at the 2nd Marine Aircraft Wing, Cherry Point, North Carolina.

Miss Mary, the ghost of a seventy-year-old woman, was first sighted in 1947. Since then, many Marines have met and talked with the apparition. What is most disturbing is that her appearances took place in a top-security area of a military base, an area that would be nearly impossible for intruders to reach.

One of the Marines who claims to have seen her, Sgt. James B. Segura, was so unnerved after his meeting with Miss Mary that he sought medical tests to confirm what happened.

Segura was on guard duty the night of November 11, 1975, when he swears he was approached by an apparition. "At least, I'd call it an apparition, in a military area surrounded by double-mesh fences and illuminated floodlights. Miss Mary was wearing a long-sleeved calico dress. She just came around this place where we had some oil drums stacked up and walked up to me," Segura said.

"My first reaction was to yell for the sergeant of the guard, but there was no one else in the area. And she looked harmless. I had this eerie feeling, because she reminded me of my own late grandmother, and she was so out of place amid all our gear."

"The woman asked my name," Segura said, "identified herself as Mary, and remarked that the weather was remarkably pleasant. She said she lived on a chicken farm nearby, but that her family soon would be forced to move. She was completely friendly, but I started to get this spooky feeling, and I decided I'd better report her to someone. I asked her to wait a minute and walked to the nearest guardpost to get my supervisor. When we came back, she was gone."

After this, Segura could not get the encounter out of his mind. Finally, he asked to be examined by the doctors at the base. They did so and determined he was neither the victim of a hoax, nor had he suffered a hallucination. In time, Segura was honorably discharged.

Segura's commanding officer supported his story. "I'm absolutely convinced that this young man had exactly the experience he describes—though I can't find any explanation for it." M. Sgt. Ronald. B. Palmer said.

Dr. Louis A. Nabb of Washington, D.C., a sociologist and researcher who studies unknown phenomena, was called in to investigate. He questioned Segura and several other Marines who had reportedly seen Miss Mary over the years. Nabb also studied local history in an effort to get to the bottom of the matter. In doing so, he discovered there had been chicken farms in the area during the 1890s, when the government purchased the land for a training base that later became the air station.

"According to the legend, an elderly woman who'd lost her husband was forced to leave the only home she'd ever known and died shortly thereafter—from heartbreak as much as anything else," explained Dr. Nabb. "If you believe the legend, she keeps returning to her old homestead, which is now a military stockpile."

The first sightings of Miss Mary occurred more than fifty years ago, and she is still seen, roughly once every six months. The Marines who have seen and talked to her all claim that her manner is curious, but not hostile.

Says Segura, "I think of her often. In a nice way."

The 2nd Marine Aircraft Wing, at Cherry Point, North Carolina, is an air station that currently accommodates about 15,000 Marines. The air station is on the Neuse River and part of the Croatan National Forest, and the closest town is Havelock, due south; the closest city, New Bern, is about a thirty-minute drive northwest.

You won't find Cherry Point on a North Carolina map, as it is not a town, but solely a Marine base. A close examination of a North Carolina atlas will reveal MARINE CORPS AIR STATION, which is the haunted base.

T HE GLASS-

TOPPED CASKET

Restaurants and gift shops are named after her. Locals lean over, and in their best storytelling voices, forewarn tourists about her. At present, students of Horry-Georgetown Technical College can take a continuing education class to learn about her. Just who is this mystery lady?

She's no secret to longtime Low Country residents. Alice Flagg is one of South Carolina's most well-known ghosts, and no book on Carolina ghosts would be complete without telling her story.

Alice was a sixteen-year-old girl who, in the 1840s, resided at the Hermitage, a house in Murrells Inlet. Legend has it she fell in love with a young man who her father did not think was a suitable mate. Alice secretly became engaged to her suitor and wore the ring he gave her on a necklace that she hid underneath her blouses and dresses.

Her secret was discovered when the girl fell ill with fever while away at school in Charleston and was consequently brought home to Hermitage. Alice's mother discovered the ring, and she showed it to her husband and son. Alice's brother responded by angrily flinging it into the nearby marsh. Despite Alice's pleas, no one tried to retrieve her ring, and in fact, she was told she would not be allowed to continue seeing her beloved.

The teen died soon thereafter, and it is reported that this was more from a broken heart than a legitimate illness.

Over the years, the ghost of Alice Flagg has been seen by many as she wanders the area, perhaps searching for her ring or her lover. Ghost hunters currently flock to the area in hopes of seeing this spirit, but they have their work cut out for them, since no one knows exactly where to look. Sightings reportedly have occurred at three different locations in Pawleys Island and Murrells Inlet.

One popular place for haunt hunters is the Old Gunn Church, in the Plantersville section of Georgetown County, near US 701 South. All that remains of the church is its tower, which resembles a castle. The crumbling structure is a popular stop for those searching for Alice Flagg, as many believe this is her final resting place. But, local historian Catherine Lewis tells her students she believes Alice is not buried at Old Gunn Church. The confusion is understandable enough. Alice Flagg's niece, Alice Belin Flagg, is buried there. The descendant's grave is marked, and it is next to tombs of other Flagg family members. A gravestone reveals Alice Belin Flagg was born in 1849, the same year her aunt died. Ironically, she died an old maid, because her father didn't approve of her true love. Her father was also the brother of the first Alice Flagg, the one who had thrown the engagement ring into the marsh. One ghost-hunting class attempted to see this grave on April 14, 1998, but was unsuccessful.

"When we were on our way, our van conked off," said Shirley Long Johnson, assistant dean of continuing education at Horry-Georgetown Technical College. "They sent another van, and that van's battery went dead as soon as it pulled up behind us. We figured Alice was trying to tell us something and just didn't want to be found."

As the group sat in the "dead" van, Catherine Lewis added to the eerie experience by telling her students another spooky tale. The contractor who helped to build the Old Gunn Church was a man named Gunn (the church is named after him), and he was a drinking man. It is said that as he was putting slates on the roof, he fell off, and his curses and screams can still be heard at certain times.

So, where is Alice Flagg buried? Many believe it is at All Saints Waccamaw Episcopal Church, in Pawleys Island. The grave is simply marked ALICE, so no one knows if this is indeed the now-famous Alice Flagg. That doesn't stop ghost hunters, who walk backwards thirteen times around the grave, trying to conjure up her spirit. Carnations, roses, and even a tiny gold ring have been left on the grave as a tribute to Alice.

Clarke Willcox Jr., whose family bought the Hermitage in 1910, said that when Alice died she was buried in a glass-topped casket at the Hermitage, and she was later moved to Cedar Hill Cemetery, presumably when the Hermitage was moved. No one can ask Willcox how he knows it was a glass-topped casket, since he died in 1989. Because of his adamant statements, many declare Alice's final resting place to be at Cedar Hill. Catherine Lewis also believes this to be true and takes her class to this cemetery as part of their quest to find Alice Flagg. "They say that Alice is buried here under this tree in an unmarked grave. This makes sense to me, because she lived a mile or so up the highway and other family members are buried here. That's what the church records say, and I guess this is as close as I've come to finding her. . . ."

The word *hermitage* means a retreat; a hideaway. The Flagg family home was built on Murrells Inlet, and it still remains there, but it was moved to a different street. The original site now contains a housing development, also called the Hermitage. The former dwelling of Alice Flagg is now a private residence, and it is not open to the public.

RESOURCES

NORTH CAROLINA

North Carolina State Chamber of Commerce
P.O. Box 2508
Raleigh, NC 27602
(919) 836-1400
www.nccbi.org

North Carolina Travel and Tourism Division
Department of Commerce
301 N. Wilmington Street
Raleigh, NC 27601
(919) 733-4171 or (800) 787-0670
www.nccommerce.com/tourism

SOUTH CAROLINA

South Carolina State Chamber of Commerce
1201 Main Street, Suite 1810
Columbia, SC 29201
(803) 799-4601
www.sccc.org

South Carolina Parks, Recreation, and Tourism
1205 Pendleton Street
Edgar Brown Building, Room 505
Columbia, SC 29201
(803) 734-0122 or (800) 962-6261 (toll-free number only for brochure requests)
www.discoversouthcarolina.com

If you enjoyed reading this book, here are some other books from Pineapple Press on related topics. For a complete catalog, write to Pineapple Press, P.O. Box 3889, Sarasota, Florida 34230, or call (800) 746-3275. Or visit our website at www.pineapplepress.com. For more information on Terrance Zepke's books and future projects, see www. terrancezepke.com.

Best Ghost Tales of North Carolina, Second Edition, by Terrance Zepke. The actors of Carolina's past linger among the living in this thrilling collection of ghost tales. Use Zepke's tips to conduct your own ghost hunt. (pb)

Best Ghost Tales of South Carolina by Terrance Zepke. The actors of Carolina's past linger among the living in this thrilling collection of ghost tales. Use Zepke's tips to conduct your own ghost hunt. (pb)

Ghosts and Legends of the Carolina Coasts by Terrance Zepke. More spine-chilling tales and fascinating legends from the coastal regions of North and South Carolina. (pb)

Coastal North Carolina by Terrance Zepke. The author visits the Outer Banks and the Upper and Lower Coasts to bring you the history and heritage of coastal communities, main sites and attractions, sports and outdoor activities, lore and traditions, and more. (pb)

Coastal South Carolina by Terrance Zepke. From Myrtle Beach to Beaufort, South Carolina's Lowcountry is steeped in history and full of charm, and author Terrance Zepke makes sure you don't miss any of it. A must-have for vacationers, day-trippers, armchair travelers, and people looking to relocate to the area. (pb)

Lighthouses of the Carolinas by Terrance Zepke. Eighteen lighthouses aid mariners traveling the coasts of North and South Carolina. Here is the story of each, from origin to current status, along with visiting information and photos. (pb)

Lowcountry Voodoo: Beginner's Guide to Tales, Spells and Boo Hags by Terrance Zepke. Learn more about voodoo with this compilation of some of the beliefs, special spells, and remarkable stories passed down through generations of families who have made their home in the South Carolina and Georgia Lowcountry. (pb)

Pirates of the Carolinas for Kids by Terrance Zepke. The Carolinas had more than their share of pirates, including Calico Jack, Billy Lewis, Long Ben Avery; and two women, Anne Bonny and Mary Read. Ages 9 and up. (pb)

Lighthouses of the Carolinas for Kids by Terrance Zepke. The history of and facts about lighthouses along the Carolina coasts. Includes color photos and illustrations, ghost stories, and a quiz. Ages 9 and up. (pb)